Reading and loving

Leila Berg

Routledge & Kegan Paul
London, Henley and Boston

First published in 1977
by Routledge & Kegan Paul Ltd
39 Store Street,
London WC1E 7DD,
Broadway House,
Newtown Road,
Henley-on-Thames,
Oxon RG9 1EN and
9 Park Street,
Boston, Mass. 02108, USA
Set in Monotype Imprint
and printed in Great Britain by
Cox & Wyman Ltd, London, Reading and Fakenham

ISBN 0 7100 8475 7 (c)
ISBN 0 7100 8476 5 (p)

Contents

Kit, Martha and Emily

Kit is – at the time of writing – my youngest grandchild.

For the first few months of his life, he and his parents, and I, were living in different parts of the same house.

He came here from the maternity home when he was three weeks old. For perhaps two weeks after that he would wake with a roaring scream, a vibrating machine-note that crashed its demand through the building. Then his cry changed – because his relationship with his environment had changed. His voice was noticeably lower; it was melodious and sad. No longer a violent demand, but a trusting and reproachful plea. No longer a savage assault on an unknown terrifying hunger-hurting world, but a communication to someone who could be trusted to give nourishment and comfort. Grief had entered his life, because of this growing relationship. It was almost a *looking at* dependency, an awareness of it, rather than the first rigid raging terror of it.

This difference in a cry was a result of a whole month's experience of dependable response, a result of Jenny coming in to him and talking gently and laughing softly, and picking him up, stroking him, touching him, still talking, and giving him what he had said he felt he needed, in close physical intimacy. (I called Jenny 'Nina' in *Look at Kids*, Penguin, 1972.)

A little later and he had started to croon back to her, gazing at her gravely while holding his first conversations, laughing soundlessly at her voice when something was said to him with laughter in it, very different from the wildness and inaccessibility of his original cries when he hadn't yet learnt trust. He had moved from a cry, to a cry and response, and then moved still further to a conversation.

A little later, when he was perhaps two and a half months, feeding at the breast, his hands would explore her body, her hair, her clothes – the territory within reach – while his bright eyes searched the room, drinking it in as his mouth drank in the milk, eagerly getting further information, while his mouth securely held on to the breast. (If you had pulled his face away from this security and confidence and trust, in which all his senses were pleasurably at work, surely he would have been thrown into great anxiety, and all his lively eagerness to explore what was farther afield would have exploded into chaos?)

At four months he recognised with delight tunes that had regularly, at definite times, been sung to him, and at the first familiar musical phrase his mouth would open upward and downward in that extraordinary rose-petal laugh of babyhood, then spread across in a happy grin; then he would join in, very seriously, leaving no doubt whatever that the tune he so solemnly improvised was participation. At this age, too, when he made one of his intriguing noises and Jenny imitated it back, he would gaze at her entranced at this mutuality, then laugh with delight.

Jenny used to carry him around for a few minutes at a time and show him different objects in the room – flowers, pictures, books – and talk to him about them. Very soon he too began to talk and comment on them. A light hangs over his parents' bed, shaded in a large sphere, purple, blue and green; this light is one of his first loves, almost on a par with Jenny, though it gives him nothing except visual pleasure. From his first days he was often laid, awake, on this bed, and gazing upwards always saw this light – sometimes on and sometimes off – and began to talk to it, and later to laugh to it. Always he reminded me of T. E. Brown's poem about the blackbird and the star, and I found myself thinking 'Good Lord! she is so bright tonight!' At five months old, when he was sitting on Jenny's lap with his back to 'his light', he would bend his body over and backwards, in order to stare, upside down and absorbedly and for a long time, at this very dear friend, often also conversing with it. (Jenny didn't jerk him round or pull him upright, but would say 'Oh, you want to talk to your light, do you?' and wait till he had finished this 'meeting'.) It was by then falling to bits, and Jenny, respecting its importance, was worried a little how they would take it with them when they moved without reducing it to dust.

She took care from the beginning that as he lay in his cot in his own room, whatever was at his eye-level on the wall or by his bed – posters, pictures, a mobile, a frieze – was colourful and interesting to him. If it is something he gazes at, talks to, laughs to, she leaves it there; if it isn't she takes it away and puts something else there and watches to see if it pleases or absorbs him, since he cannot yet initiate his own choices. Because she had always drawn his attention to such things, he was, while still very tiny, interested in the colour of people's clothes; he gazed at them, talked about them, fingered them, gathered them up, tried to screw them into his mouth; if the clothes were worn by Jenny, instead of moving away or loosening his fingers she would move nearer.

From the time he was four months old, and going out in his pram lying still mainly flat so that his vision was skyward, he so gazed at, and conversed with, the trees, that you felt that his next toy should be a shady tree that could stand near his cot with a piece of blue sky and a cloud tied to the top. And a tree in blossom – for this has been a freak winter, and all the spring blossom was out in January – so affected him that he panted with excitement, fists clenching and unclenching, and could not speak for ecstasy.

At four to five months he had already framed the idea of expectancy and association. When you took his vest over his head, he reasonably shut his eyes tight and screwed up his face; so when you took his vest over his arms, he did the same – shut his eyes and screwed up his face. We always thought this was funny – but how his intelligence was working, to remember and apply!

If you make a noise now, with your fingers curled up in the air ready for a tickly pounce, he will gasp the next time you make the noise, waiting, eyes sparkling, for the pounce, and will laugh with joy as this expectation is confirmed.

I remember I talked to him when he was about four months, just tossed him a sentence, and he shouted with laughter, which made *me* laugh, and that made *him* laugh again, and so we went on, just catching each other's eye and collapsing with laughter. This is something that generally happens with a friend of one's own age: it was odd to notice suddenly that this sharer of completely relaxed laughter was a four-month-old baby.

By five months, you could already play 'Round and round the garden' with him, tickling his palm very solemnly and quietly, walking up his arm with your fingers and tickling under his chin, watching his gleeful anticipation, his delighted apprehension – sure in his anxiety and suspense that pleasure would crown the sequence. This is a mini-plot that he was following. At five months, this baby was dipping a toe into stories.

An interesting thing has happened recently, his sixth to seventh month. From birth Kit has had a lullaby-bell – one of those musical boxes whose string you pull to play a lullaby – to go to sleep with. The string is pulled, then he is left alone, and goes to sleep. When he was taken on a visit, his great-grandfather took out a wooden Swiss bowl, which was actually a musical box though it played a different tune from his lullaby-bell. Instead of being delighted at the familiar sound (for he recognises the sounds of known musical instruments, as well as being delighted by music anyway) he seemed to be thrown off balance, worried and agitated. And the same thing happens if Jenny puts a second lullaby-bell, which his great-grandfather gave him and which plays the same tune as his night-time one, in his pram, and plays it while they are out, when he seems bored or tired; he gets agitated instead of being soothed. Perhaps – for his hearing, so pleasantly nurtured, is very sensitive – he is disturbed that that kind of sound which he knows so well should come out of an unexpected object. Or perhaps he can't yet accept a musical box, whatever the tune, outside the bedtime situation where it has always belonged. It will be interesting to see when he can accept that this sound, which he has already grown old enough to identify and is so tranquilly satisfied to recognise in its 'right place', has a relaxed right to turn up anywhere and anytime. I find it fascinating to see in this baby how each step in growth alters the current situation which has only recently been understood and accepted by the baby and docketed in his memory – how grief enters one step ahead of joy.

I worry because neither of his lullaby-bells which both play the Brahms lullaby, play it correctly. I bought one, his great-grandfather the other. Each plays a truncated version, commercial practicality being more important than musical beauty or integrity. Will he, perhaps never knowing why, be disturbed when as an adult he hears it played correctly? And did he cry in his pram because the wrong one he heard was different from the wrong one he knew? And the bowl, which pretended to be making the same kind of sound, was playing a tune that wasn't even *remotely* like the tune he knew; it was even wronger! Perhaps his anxiety had nothing to do with the dishonoured association of time, or of object, but with the dishonoured association of sound? Certainly, he has become old enough and experienced enough to make associations and remember and have expectations; and this again brings disappointment and shock and grief before it brings extended delight. Soon he will be old enough perhaps to accept, with the help he has, that one needn't hold so *tight* to one's expectations, that it is pleasurable to move beyond, or without, expectations. . . .

At eight months, after Frank, his father, had played 'Knock at the door, ring the bell' with him, for the first time he did it again *himself*, knocking on his forehead, pulling his ear, touching his nose, opening his mouth and putting his finger in. He did it very tentatively, obviously both remembering and exploring (both drawing from the past and moving into the future), in very much the same way as, at the same time, he suddenly began poking with one extended finger at a crust of bread which before he would simply have clutched with his hand – as if familiar things had suddenly revealed an unexpectedness or a variety that said they should no longer be taken for granted but carefully investigated. On the same day he initiated and created two separate varieties of 'Peep-bo' entirely on his own, insisting on having a partner and getting a serious delight from this self-chosen collaboration. In these three instances on this one day, he deliberately and on his own initiative shared the delight that his body provided with another person – gave a present to someone who had given him presents.

And now he is also beginning to put food into your mouth. This for me is the essence of human growth, this delight in *mutuality*, this wanting to give that is sparked off by being given to (and that is killed by our school system).

For a little while now he has been blowing raspberries – he is teething, and when he is given a spoonful of dinner he sometimes blows it out with a spattering noise. Jenny was not enthusiastic about it. After considering the situation, she raised her eyebrows, waved a finger at him, and said 'No'. He fell about with laughter. Now he has instituted another game: he puts his mouth ready to blow a raspberry, Jenny raises her eyebrows, lifts her finger, and puts her mouth ready to say 'No' – and he collapses in helpless laughter. And so does Jenny. (Weeks before, he would laugh whenever anyone pulled a funny face – even if it was only raising an eyebrow or screwing up their mouth. How is a baby so definite that this is not the usual face, and how does he know it is meant to be funny? Already this baby is busy classifying, and having classified successfully – for the time being – knows when something has broken the rule, and is – sometimes – able to laugh, not to worry, about it.)

There is an empty house up the road, with masses of lilac in the garden. A month or so ago, Jenny went up in the evening and brought an armful back. She set these luscious trusses in a bowl on the left of the living-room window. In the morning Kit was ecstatically excited about this – not only the sight of the lilac, but also, we thought, the scent. Every time he was carried into the room he gazed at the lilac, and talked to it. One evening Jenny went up to the empty house again, brought back more, and set it on the television set on the right of the window. Next morning Kit was brought into the living-room, and as usual gazed immediately at his flowers on the left. At last, with a half-sigh he turned his face away – and suddenly caught sight of the others. He was visibly amazed. He stared, as if he just could not credit it. Then he turned his head to the left. The lilac was still there. Then to the right. Still there. On and on he went, turning his head from side to side like someone watching a tennis match. He seemed to be wondering if it was the *same* bowl of flowers changing its place, whether perhaps he could competently catch it in the very act of moving from one place to another. Or was it remotely possible – and this would be a new step forward in experience – that there could be *two* bowls of lilac? Again, it was memory, and classification (flowers belonging on *that* table), with something sensuously important to him involved.

At eight and a half months, an absolutely new thing happened with him. He would turn and look at the lilac, if you said 'Where are your flowers?' He would turn and locate his fish too if you said 'Where are your fishes?' (These are a mobile, which he and Jenny always gaze at and talk about when he goes to bed. If he woke in the evening distressed from teething, she would lift him up and show him his fishes, and talk about them, and he would be comforted.) He looked at his tea-time banana too, if you said 'Where's your banana?' These three things – on which he had fixed a definite verbal label – were all very dear to him.

Today he is eleven months old.

Months ago he was in love with a light. 'Ka' he said to it, with a lot of 'h' in it – 'kha' – a soft breath of tender wonder. When they moved, worrying that he would feel the loss, he seemed to forget about it, as inseparable playmates in nursery school forget about each other when they move on; so many new experiences, activities, learnings have been filling his life.

But today he has suddenly discovered lights again, not just one particular light hanging from the ceiling like his old love, but lights everywhere – pendant lights, standing lamps, bedside table lamps, traffic lights, even the little light inside the car; all become 'Kha' again – as have also two mobiles *that hang from the ceiling*. After all this time, he has suddenly reached back for a past achievement that now seems to him suitable for further use and development. 'Kha' now means for him not just one particular loved pendant light, but a *class*, both of things that glow, and things that hang from the ceiling. Later on, he will divide this classification further. It is amazing how much classification a baby embarks on, and completes, of his own accord, long before schooldays. And equally amazing how even at this very early age, he reaches back into his past and re-connects, in order to move on.

He now uses this same one consonant for everything he names. Jenny, who is an actress and studied phonetics, can distinguish the different words, and knows, if she is in another room, what particular 'Ka' word he is calling. 'Ka-ka', said in a particular way, is 'curtain'. He goes to the curtain at the side of the window, says 'Ka-ka' – gazing at you intently – then goes to the other one and does the same. He will do the same in any room he enters where there are curtains; and I know he would be very distressed if he ever found himself in a room where there wasn't a pair.

In the morning, when he first wakes from his night-time sleep and holds intimate conversations in the half-light with his teddy-bear, holding him confidentially by one ear and putting his cheek against him (he has lately become very fond of his soft toys. Earlier he was interested in harder things that he manipulated, using mouth, hand, fingers; now he wants things to cuddle and talk to, and the cuddling must surely be part of what he is saying) and again in his exploratory vocalising, he uses many different sounds. He is particularly fond at the moment of a tongue-clicking sound that makes him laugh when Jenny and Frank do it to him; and he practises it on his own.

But when he is united with adults he quite deliberately limits his sounds, to the one he has decided is part of your language, and says it in a quite different way, looking at you as he speaks, gravely or enquiringly, to make clear he is communicating with you, and isn't fooling. 'Ka-ka', he says to you. 'Yes. Curtain', you reply, enunciating clearly. 'Ka-ka', he says, obviously duplicating.

He repeats rhythm, at least, he says 'Ka-ka' when you say 'Curtain'. Earlier, an aeroplane was 'ka-ka' which distinguished it from a car, which was 'ka'. Has he clung to this one syllable because when he first said it we delightedly 'recognised' it as 'car', so that joyfully he gives us the sound we applaud and thinks it is the magic word for everything? Perhaps one can say he can count to two. Certainly he is very aware of two curtains. Perhaps this began when he was about seven months old, and became aware of two vases of flowers, and fully experienced and practised this awareness. So many things go with the development of speech, and all long, long before a child goes to school.

I sent these observations to a young mother whose baby – her fourth child – had been born about the same time as Kit. I was intrigued by her reply. Here is this baby Matthew:

> I can't remember timings exactly. But at about a couple of months old, Matthew would interrupt a breast feed frequently to communicate; he would 'coo' for quite long periods and showed strong displeasure if I looked away or tried to encourage him to continue his feed. I remember the yell of reproachful rage I would get if I tried to release his teeth (he had his first at three months) from my breast. He just could not come to terms with his warm friendly mother trying to part him, somewhat rapidly, from his source of food!
>
> He used to sleep on his stomach and so I put a couple of transfers on the backboard of the cot right down at sheet level. Often when we went to fetch him at three months he would be 'talking' earnestly at the kitten or the panda. He seemed to prefer the panda perhaps because he had large black eyes!
>
> At four to five months he too responded to 'Round and

round the garden'. It was interesting to notice that he would chuckle and screw himself up in anticipation at the *words* of the rhyme not only with the associated actions. He did in fact seem to understand many more words than one would expect. It's often only a change in direction of a glance that reveals the understanding. I'm sure that I have noticed far more with Matthew than I did with the others.

At five or six months if we laid him on the bed and asked him where the clock was he would roll himself round to look at it. He also recognised certain things such as spoon, keys, cup.

At seven to eight months I used to experiment a little with him. I would put down on the floor (he was crawling then) a number of toys and would watch him playing with them. When I had noticed him touch and play with say, a car, then lose interest and go on to something else, I would then ask him where the car was. He didn't always return to the car but his eyes would flutter round to where it was. If I asked him before he had played with the object he was not able to search through the toys to find it (with his eyes, I mean) even though he clearly understood the word.

To return to Kit – yes, he repeats rhythm, and pitch, but not the actual consonant; he is concentrating just now on the *emotional feel* of communication which is exactly what children a little older do when they come to writing and to reading, in natural loving conditions. He isn't yet ready to repeat individual sounds as adults say them; he will do it in his own time.

I remember a year or two ago when Emily, another grandchild, used to point to parts of her body and name them – 'Nose', 'chin', 'eye' – she would stick her thumb out of her fist and say 'Bumb'. 'Th-th-thumb' I would say, with my tongue thrust exaggeratedly between my teeth. 'Bumb!' she would repeat, with enthusiastic co-operation. She stayed with me for a few days, and I concentrated very hard on teaching her to say 'Th'; energetically she stuck her tongue between her teeth and spluttered through, and I was triumphant. Dan and Su came back just as this was accomplished. I said, showing off, 'What's this, Emily?' – holding up my thumb – 'Put your tongue between your teeth.' 'Th-th-th-th-BUMB', she said with gusto.

Chapter 1

I learned – as I have often done before but keep forgetting – not to push Nature. Self-importance gets in the way. I sometimes wonder how much we stop children learning things by teaching them, instead of making it more and more possible for them to teach themselves. She is now working her way towards 'thumb' by currently saying 'Flumb' – and, when an adult gets helpful, 'Th-th-th-flumb!'

Later, up in Lancashire, I sat in the living-room with Emily, Martha (nearly five), and Debra from next door aged six. Everyone was writing letters. Martha – of her own choice – was writing to Beryl, whom she'd never met but who had sent her a lolly by me, Debra was writing to her Great Grandma, Emily (two and a half) who had also been sent a lolly by Beryl, was writing not to her but to Jenny, whom she *had* met. Debra, who had been at school a year, and who was very eager to write ('Dear Great Grandma', she wanted to say, 'When will you come and visit Grandma so we can come across the road to you?') couldn't manage any of the words for herself, and Martha kept leaning across to her and spelling everything for her in an extremely competent and bossy way, so that, finding my role slipping and perhaps also afraid that this might affect Martha's own letter badly (two anxieties which must also be frequent with teachers!), I began to get irritated . . . 'You look after your own letter, Martha! *I'll* help Debra!'

Emily was scribbling away, at one picture after another, all for Jenny. When each time I asked what she wanted me to write on the bottom of them, it was just 'For Jenny, for Jenny, for Jenny!' as if simply the act of communicating was intensity enough. Martha's letter which she wrote entirely on her own, and which was very clear until she covered it with 142 kisses, was this:

> Dear Beryl
>   I have a wobbly toof
> ti is very very wobbly
> I wondr wen it's going to
> come out
> Fank you for the lollies
>   Love for MARTHA

At nearly 5, Martha who had an extensive vocabulary and also wrote well, was writing 'f' for 'th' – 'Fank you' and 'my toof'. Anyone reading her letters would have assumed either that she lived among Cockneys in London, or that she couldn't pronounce 'th'. In fact, the accent around her was broad Lancashire, and she pronounced 'th' perfectly – she read back her 'Fank you' as 'Thank you'. I was perplexed. I suppose her silent speech (writing) had not yet reached the same discriminating power as her vocalised speech. Perhaps one doesn't often meet discrepancies like this because children usually begin to write after all this has clarified.

None of these three children – Martha, Emily, Kit – is five yet. Kit is not even one. In fact he is a person whom many will consider still very far from *talking*; they will say that language only starts when a dictionary word is spoken; and Kit has not yet spoken one. If you query this assumption, they will tell you that language is communication; to which you can only answer that communication depends on the mutuality of two people; and where one person makes a sound and the other responds in the hoped-for way to that sound, then you have language. *A person who does not respond in this way prevents the sound from becoming language.* By the time some children are five years old and come to school, they have been engaged in language for a full five years; others have been so engaged for only three, others for one perhaps, some for scarcely any time at all.

I have come further than I meant to. It is because I have not been able to pull my attention away from Kit, and Kit, like all babies, has developed so fast. All I meant to show in this chapter was how this baby emphasised for me my feeling that when a child has confidence that an adult has things to offer that are pleasurably and sensually satisfying, even though sometimes a bit of waiting, or work, or anxiety, real or playful, must be gone through first, and when a child believes that he himself has something intensely loving to offer that will be accepted with love, and when at the meeting-point of these two offerings a delight is formed, he comes naturally and healthily to communication, to stories, and, I believe, to writing and reading.

Round and round the garden

Why do we have to call 'Round and round the garden' a 'finger-play?' Such a clinical, professional, and therefore alienating word, no-one but an academic could possibly know what it means. Isn't it just a nursery rhyme, or, if we want to be more specific, a nursery tickle rhyme? I shall call such rhymes 'tickle rhymes' from now on.

What tickle rhymes do to a baby like Kit is not just to delight, and not only to set memory and anticipation going, either. They make to the unacademic but very aware baby three important and different statements. They say something objective: 'This is you. Feel my touch. I am outlining the outside of you. This is you, snugly safe under my hand; and beyond is the outside world.' (Anyone who has watched a baby concentratedly bite a teething ring, and then with the same exploring concentration bite his toe – the bewilderment, shock, grief, pain, rage, that roll down his face like a window-blind! – knows how confused we all are at the beginning about what is us, and what is something else. Some of us are never sure of it all our lives, and many of us at least have bad times when we lose track. Perhaps we were never tickled enough?)

The second thing they say is also about the baby's identity, but it is emotional. Because of the laughing, loving tone of voice, and the playful touch, the tickle rhyme says not only 'This is *you*' but also '*You* are very precious, important and pleasurable to me. I share with you the delight of every part of you, every curve, every cranny. . . .'

The third thing they say is 'Words, like touch, is part of outlining you, of getting to know you more deeply and of showing you to yourself, of loving you.'

I once watched a young adult doing finger-plays – that is what she had been taught to call them of course – with nearly fifty toddlers in a day nursery. The number of adult workers there was very low at the best of times, and the only reason the dedicated matron in charge wasn't despairing or angry was that she would have felt that useless and immoral . . . perhaps wrongly? Anyway, that week the situation was worse than usual because it was winter-time and one of the two full-time workers had flu. So this girl took fifty children who were just emerging from babyhood (and who left to themselves would have formed groups of three at the most), and made them sit down round thirteen tables, four children round every table (none able to touch her, and only one out of every four even able to see her); she herself sat some way off, and after spending a lot of time trying to get these toddlers to stay in their chairs, to stop crying, to stop banging their seats or tables (all this from a distance, since to approach one out of a horde of fifty toddlers might have been disastrous, so that before she had started she was already very strained and hoarse) she began 'Round and round – sit *down*, Errol! Round – stop turning round, Mandy! Round and round the – be *quiet*, John. Sit still! *Don't* turn round to look at me!'

Sitting alone, on a straight-backed chair, touching no-one, she went through her stern finger-plays, issuing commands like a sergeant major. The kind of finger-plays she was doing were geared to fun, laughter and intimacy and above all cuddling. And as well as this, they were *symbols*, in this case the child's own fingers, hands and arms, standing for the ingredients of a story, just as later on, written letters and words will stand for the ingredients of a story; the child would have been using his own loved identity to playfully tell a story. But no-one had ever explained to this girl what finger-plays were about; and if they had how could she ever have cuddled fifty little children? So what was this rhyme supposed to be doing for them, these toddlers who left home every morning before it was even light and returned in the dark? Was it just The Right Thing – 'The Way It Spozed to Be', in James Herndon's phrase?

One day I did 'Round and round the garden' to a little group – not fifty! – a baby under a year, a baby of just one year, a child of three and a half, and a child of four and a half, two of them strangers to me.

You reach out and take a strange child's hand – and you get this suspicious frowning at you from under the eyebrows, this furrowed brow, perhaps a pulling away of the hand at a stranger's invasion of privacy. And you hold on to the hand, not frighteningly, *gently*, and you say, 'Wait . . . *Round and round the garden like a teddy-bear*' – describing circles on the child's reluctantly open palm. And the child looks down, and *feels* the feeling. And this feeling flows through him like wine, and his defences melt away while you wait. And when you *see* they have melted away, and a face of delight and wonder is turned up to you, you go on. 'One step, two steps and *tickle* you under there.' 'Again! Again!' the children shriek, while the one-year-old shouts his one syllable and waves his hand under your nose, and the baby makes an urgent whimpering and waving and wriggling. This magic ritual – the combination of physical touch with sound – has worked. But who could do this one at a time with fifty?

Three together

Kit was born, like another grandchild, in a very small natural childbirth maternity home (The Family Maternity Home) where two mothers stay at a time, where fathers and other children in the families come and stay, and fathers can actively help with the birth and where the midwife who runs it has already become a personal friend from previous visits.

I know that a baby born here will be laid on his mother's naked, exultant body, still himself naked, slimy and bloody, the umbilical cord still pulsating and uncut between them, and that as he draws in his first air and shouts with life his mother will hold him, skin to skin, heart to heart, half-crying perhaps with the overwhelming joy of hard achievement. I know that the father may have actively helped with the delivery so that her achievement – and the baby's – was also his, and riding through difficulties and effort and pain into triumphant vitality and tenderness has been inextricably interlinked for all three of them. And there has been nothing academic or clinical about this; real bodies have worked and sweated at it, and held each other. So from the very outset, at such a birth sound goes with vitality, with discovery, with exultation, with the deeply-felt and hotly physical experience of private individuals.

When the mother and baby leave this home three weeks after the birth, they are sharing breast feeding, and also sharing the natural rhythm of the particular baby's sleep. For Olive Rogers, who runs this Home, says it takes a full three weeks for the mother to have become aware of her own baby's sleep rhythm, and to have noted where her baby's longest sleep regularly falls, and to have gently nudged and pulled this long sleep little by little into the night-time period when we all want rest.

How many thousands of mothers would love their babies spontaneously, how many parents and babies would be more vital and creative and enjoy life together, if the exploding, splintered nights they experienced had been instead restful, because they had trusted, and learned how to confidently extend, the baby's own rhythm? Wouldn't this be worth teaching in maternity hospitals, to bring home a baby who sleeps all night?

Under this tutelage, Kit's crying was listened to, and the different meanings behind it discovered, which meant too that for Kit *communication early became successful* because what was said was understood and truly responded to; he was not filled with milk when he was speaking of something else until he finally became confused *himself* about what he was communicating. Day by day his growth and his growing needs were wondered about and recognised with pleasure; with the result that his 'time-table' – except for that gradual edging of his long sleep into the night-time which he co-operated with – was entirely his own, and yet was never burdensome. From very early on, dialogue had been established.

(To follow a baby's natural rhythm is not a chaotic stupefying business. Both authoritarians and child-centred people tend to think it is – the first repressively, the second patiently – because their own childhood gave them such a low opinion of themselves. But one has to *learn* to do it since it wasn't done to oneself in childhood, learn to perceive the baby's order.)

During their three-week stay, the three of them received belief in themselves, joy in each other, and a confidence in dialogue. If we all had this, many of the institutions of our society would break down or be dismantled. Also, I believe, to return to my theme, children would read with ease. For I believe reading is concerned precisely with these things – belief in yourself, joy in each other, and confidence in dialogue.

Words and welcomes

By now, many teachers, having picked up this book in the hope that it might solve their most urgent problems, will be saying 'My God, it was bad enough in her previous writing when she wanted us to mother the children! Now she wants us to deliver the babies too!'

I'm not actually asking that. I'm only asking teachers, as well as all other people, to look at the whole situation. In any case, I'm afraid there is more to come. For an important thing about Kit, something that has already fed into this baby's confidence, vitality and intelligence, is that he was wanted. To want a baby is not, as some people are currently professing to believe, a matter of will, or self-discipline; clenched hands don't tickle well.

Kit was conceived, grew to full term, and was born, because his parents felt confident enough in themselves, in each other, and in their duality, to consolidate it all with a baby; they believed they had something good to offer to the baby, and that the baby had something good to offer them. Until they felt they had reached this point of maturity they were able to avoid giving birth to a baby.

I wonder how many children sitting today in the nation's classrooms were welcomed by their parents – let alone welcomed by their teachers, or society as a whole. The ones who were are the ones who have confidence in themselves and in others. And I suspect that the ones who had at least one of these three welcomes, are the uu-neurotic readers.

Open Sesame!

I must leave Kit, who is after all only eight months old, and write and speak of children in general. (From now on, except where I speak of a specific child, the pronoun 'he' or 'she' covers both girl and boy.)

Simply to show most clearly the ideas that have occupied me for so long, let me present the lives – bookwise – of children from two quite different homes. The children are imaginary, in that probably no child exists whose total circumstances are exactly like either of these two. But like the characters in books, each is made up from bits of real children observed, having real experiences in real environments.

The first is a baby whose home is full of books. They are not only on the shelves but scattered on the chairs and on the floor, for this is a home where books are an accepted and inherited part of life, not a strain or a striving. There are pictures on the wall, attractive colours and textures, plenty of space both indoors and out, flowers, music.

This baby is sung to, and talked to, stroked and patted and tickled to old rhymes . . . 'Apple pie, apple pie, Baby loves apple pie and so do I!' . . . so that he literally feels his lovableness.

Very early on he begins to comment on his life, using sounds not just for demand or protest, but for a sort of musing grunting melody that accompanies his satisfactions. Feeding at the breast he will become a one-man band, . . . with the steady noisy rhythm of his sucking, the rhythmic clenching and unclenching of his fingers, the rhythmic beating of his fist on his mother's body, and then, added to this percussion, to this ground base, a steady hum . . .

Perhaps a baby who 'sings' himself and is also sung to by other people, absorbs an understanding that other people too have feelings and express them in sound, and so very early develops an imaginative sensitivity. A mother of several children rocking a quiet baby lets her mind wander to her own preoccupations; and if for the baby's waking hours one tries to produce only joys, the sadnesses collected together will be waiting for attention when the baby is quiet, though perhaps not yet asleep. (Isla Cameron, the folk-singer, who once collected cradle-songs, talked on radio about the sadness that is in many of them. A large number of letters arrived for her after this broadcast, startling her with their vehemence and anger. If shattering an image was something one did more deliberately, one would know to duck.)

So such a baby babbles in his pram, unrestrained, in fact happily encouraged. Whether outside in fine weather or inside in cold, he is always within sight and hearing of the adult responsible for him though without impinging unbearably; for this baby very likely has a garden outside and a room of his own inside. And because he lives spaciously, it's unlikely that neighbours will complain of the noise he makes. If they do, because his family perhaps lives in a flat, his mother will go round and discuss it; she is fluent and skilful in the use of words and she is used to working out relationships – and although she believes other people are important, she above all believes that she and her baby are important, and she is not only sure that her first duty is to her young baby's growth, but is also confident in her ability to ensure this.

So such a baby will make all his natural noise. That's to say, this baby first will make every sound he can (and all of them are responded to). They spread widely – they are the sounds of every race, every nationality throughout the world. And they spread up and down – his pitch can cover two and a half octaves.

But he needs to talk to these particular adults who are important to him, who are more limited in sounds and in pitch, so after a while, unconsciously and voluntarily (that's to say, without being taught), he concentrates on sounds and pitches that seem to appeal most to them.

Then a magic thing happens. It is like the sound *Open Sesame*! throwing open the treasure cave. One of these sounds has a different quality. It makes something happen. It is so powerful that excitement radiates out of this room where the sound was made and love is tremendously intensified. The baby, by chance, has spoken English. Because this baby is so often *with* an adult, and because this adult is always encouraging him in conversation, his magic sound is picked up instantly and instantly gets its delighted response. It is difficult to say whose is the greater pleasure – the baby making the magic sound or the adult hearing it. So this baby learns, without tension and for the pleasure of cuddles, to select his sounds that get the magic response, and to throw away the others.

Now he goes further. Still voluntarily, and in his own time which is shaped only by his satisfying and enjoyable interaction with his own important people, he begins to imitate them. He copies the melody of their sentences (so that from his sweeping arpeggios, or his vividly-high sustained notes, he comes down to fascinatingly-accurate conversation tunes); and – a different thing – he copies their separate words. He does this, too, not because he is taught, but because he discovers for himself, in his own time, that it is relationships that make life good, and that speech, like drinking someone's milk, twining fingers in their hair, holding up your arms, is a way of enriching the bond between yourself and someone else.

Every communication this baby makes – or almost every one – is *responded* to. And this constant interchange and development continues to inform this very young baby that words are magic – words are love, acceptance, delight, cuddling.

Bodies and books

When he is only a little over a year old, you can see such a baby sitting on his mother's lap – or on the lap of another adult – looking at a picture book (because this is a family that expects even babies to delight in books). As he looks at the picture, he leans against her body, feels her warmth, her softness and firmness, and traces with his own hands and his own eyes the arms protectively around him. He does this at first passively, with that inturnedness of a baby. Then he does it again deliberately, with awareness, *choosing* to experience and explore these arms that are round him. He strokes them and gravely stares at them. Then he looks back to the book – and he listens. Then he leans back and looks, upside down, at the face that is smiling at the book and at him, and the mouth that is saying these magic sounds. He reaches a hand upwards and backwards and tries to pick out between finger and thumb the words as they come from the lips. He puts his hand over the mouth to *feel* the sounds and the breath that comes with them. Then he looks at the book again. At this point, probably, his parent or whoever holds him quite instinctively puts *him* in the book. She says 'Oh, there's a mug like Sam's. Is that Sam's mug?' 'Look, there's a cat like Sam's. Is it Sam's pussy-cat?' And so this baby is *in* this book; this is this individual baby's book. It is a book about *him* – no-one else.

All this sensuousness, playfulness, physical intimacy, protectiveness, personal identification, are part of what comes to this baby, with this very first book – just as the building up of his own loved and lovable identity rested right from the beginning on

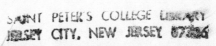

linking words with physical caresses. Words are a warm body that tickles and cuddles and holds.

As the baby begins to form first words, the magic becomes more imperious. Just as he now does not have to wait to be picked up or trundled about but can move where he himself decides to go – crawling, hitching himself, walking – so also the sounds he makes are no longer just concerned with being dependent but have *power* in them, power extending outside. You watch an eighteen-month-old baby, demanding something, or communicating something with his one deliberately selected syllable – and this syllable which means something very definite is incomprehensible to the adults. The syllable gets louder – more urgent. Then the baby adds physical gesture, more and more emphatic, more and more peremptory! till eventually the adult understands, and does what is wanted. Then the baby is satisfied, that wonderfully replete satisfaction that follows the urgent and successful effort of creation: what magic! Often an amazed delight holds his face like a sustained chord. This is very powerful communication indeed. And for its success it depends a great deal on the adult having time, not only at that precise moment, but so to speak being lapped in time always, *as far as the child is concerned*, so that even when her mind is whirling she is able at least to make a nest of calm and quiet and hovering time around the impetuous child; and of course it needs too a respect for the child, and the child's wish and ability to communicate.

This baby, for a large part of the day at least, comes first with his most important adult. So his confidence and his intelligence and his skills grow, as would any such lucky baby.

'That's me!'

When such a child is about one and a half, books are shown to him as he lies sleepy in bed, and talked over with him in the languorous, drowsy half-light, with the smell of milk and of bodies and of unfastidious teddy-bears; and they drift with him into sleep and dreams, where they become pieces of his own unconscious mythology, and play their part in his secret dramas.

And not only is the book coming right into the child's life, but the child is coming right into the book's life. For you will see him already putting his own experiences and emotions into books – coming to meet the book compiler more than halfway (sometimes far more generously than the unimaginative, limited compiler deserves).

Often too, at this time, the adult he spends his time with begins to make up stories about *him*, for this is an adult who himself was brought up with stories and is at ease with them and has relatively little self-consciousness about creating one, and is fluent in language, and enjoys the flattery of an ardent listener. So again this very young child is shown, as happens to him repeatedly in numerous ways, that he is the valid subject of stories, that books are his own life.

I remember I once sat down with Emily, then twelve months old, to look at a picture-book together. It was the kind of book I had always hunted for, for my own children – pictures of familiar things (not queens and yaks, but teddies and drinks) presented absolutely simply, on an uncluttered page. I showed Emily a picture of a spoon. I thought it would interest her because I knew she was feeding herself now, and I knew food was important to her. But it didn't interest her at all. What did interest her was a picture of a cat and a picture of a dog.

This surprised me. She didn't have a cat, or a dog, whereas she certainly had a spoon. But I hadn't realised that as it was the sort of house where friends and neighbours are constantly coming and going, and the living-room opens on to the street and stands ajar, a cat did often come in, and a dog sometimes came in, so they were in fact familiar. And they were also tremendously exciting – the physical *feel* of them – the noise they made – their movements – and this excitement that the *real living* creature evoked was transferred by the baby on to this cold flat shiny motionless page.

I had often been filled with wonder over many years at the way a baby who knows an intensely vital cat – springing, purring, throbbing, scratching, miaowing, lapping – will recognise the cat depicted on a shiny two-dimensional page which seems to me to have none of the qualities that classify CAT for a baby. I hadn't allowed for, I hadn't *recognised*, the intensely powerful bridging quality of the child's *excitement* at the original, or fully realised how much the delight that first takes one into books is an emotional re-experience.

So Emily and I looked at these pictures of DOG and CAT, which, though she couldn't say words, obviously had her riveted with excitement, and when I added sounds – barking – miaowing – she was thrown into ecstasy, and kept finding these pages, turning over the leaves purposefully, eagerly and indefatigably, in order to thrust them at me again and have me make the magic sounds that identified them, that were *remembered*, and that brought them to life. The spoon that my informative adult mind had thought was important to her was cold, clinical, lifeless, and she was indifferent to it. A spoon is not much altered by the transfer to the printed page – it is merely changed from three-dimensional to flat; it hasn't lost movement, or voice. But a cat! And yet it is precisely that very life that it seems to have lost and that therefore is supplied by the rememberer that makes it dear and exciting and involving.

By chance, a week after that I was back in London, at a hospital casualty department. I was sitting at one end of the waiting room and at the other was a small boy, aged about eighteen months, with his mother, waiting, looking at a picture book they had brought with them. As the mother and the child turned the pages, the child gazed at each one, quite ecstatically absorbed, and said BEH. His one syllable – BEH. He said this syllable, varying according apparently to the picture, with many entirely different emotions. 'Beh! Beh!' he shouted with joy, pointing. 'Ah, beh!' he grieved, over the next page, shielding it with the tender concern of his body. I sat entranced, watching him, and when a chair next to him was vacated, I crossed the room and took it, and made friends with this baby, so that after a while he decided he would show me his book. These were not pictures of bears as I had half-wondered. These were ducks. 'Beh' was his word that he used for everything, varying in a wonderfully lively way the emotion and the tone. Perhaps when he first said 'Beh', experimenting happily with sounds, his parents 'recognised' it with delight as 'bear', so he stuck to it – he had hit language! And perhaps now be believed he was using the same sound as the adults used – Duck – because he believed his emotion was creating it, was – as it is literally – the moving force.

They were ducks, I say, but they were ducks of a kind I would never have expected to find succeeding in a baby's book. They were ducks in pinafores, bonnets, scarves, with shopping bags and parasols, but without the delicate and carefully observed reality of Beatrix Potter animals – crude, pointless, *jumbled* ducks. But that child was putting into those pictures all the remembered reality of feeding real ducks on a pond – the *noise*, the splashing, the flapping, the snatching – the duck who grabs everything, and the duck who gets nothing – and that, for him, was what these pictures were to which he was responding with so much glee. (His mother, an intelligent, middle-class, book-loving mother, was disappointed in him. She thought he was backward. 'But his vitality drew me right across the room!' I protested. She said 'Well he's eighteen months, and his sister talked a lot at his age.')

I looked at this child, and remembered Emily, and I saw that the life of a one-year-old's picture book depends not only on familiarity and simplicity but on excitement, the true excitement that comes to someone who has experienced something for the very first time, and is having that emotional and physically delighting experience evoked again by the pages of a book.

By the time Emily was a year and a half she was pressing books on adults and clambering unasked on to their laps; if they lagged in opening it at a page, she did it for them; and if they sometimes politely refused to read to her she climbed down and sat on the floor, 'reading' to herself, turning over each page and naming and commenting on it.

One day when she came to visit me at this time, I jotted down forty-four actual words that she used, and I recognised, during that short space of time in my presence:

BOOK		TEDDY	
MUMMY		CHICK	
BIRD		BALLOON	
BABY		TRAIN	
CLOCK		WROTE (meaning writing	
DOG		material)	
CAT		LIGHT	
MILK	sometimes difficult	DUCK	
DRINK	to differentiate.	QUACK	
	She interchanges	COW	
	them anyway.	MOO	
DOOR		SLEEP	
CAR		TREE	
DONK (donkey)		MARTHA	
COAL		HOLE	
UP		TWO	
PRAM		BUS	
HELLO		WELLY (sometimes just WE –	
HAND		for Wellington)	
SOCK		UP-THERE	
NO		DIRTY (i.e. nappy)	
CHAIR		HOT	
COAT		BLOW	
SHOE		STEP (stair?)	

I have no idea how many other words she used by then in the more normal and relaxed course of her life, or how many she'd used that I had not recognised; I had not seen her for some months. But when Martha, her elder sister, was a year and a half, Dan (Bob, in *Look at Kids*) and Su in some curiosity jotted down all the words and phrases she used over the days, apart from friends' names. They totalled an astonishing 258. Of the 180 nouns, 37 were connected with the home, 25 with her body, 25 with food, 21 with just outside the house and 19 more with the street and a further 9 with the sky, 16 with clothes, 12 with toys, 10 with bedtime, and 6 with bathtime. Another 36 were verbs or action phrases (which they counted as one word), 26 were qualities (adjectives or adverbs), and 16 were miscellaneous exclamations. Yet I have met many teachers who believe, without necessarily putting it into words, that children only start to develop language when they come to school. It seems more likely that the teachers do not understand the language the children are using; or perhaps the children, like most adults, do not wish to talk to strangers who speak an unknown language. (I would go farther than that statement. I have met many teachers who believe children are *born* at the compulsory school-entering age.)

With the knowledge that Martha's home was a terrace house whose front room opened straight on to a steep Lancashire street, cobbled lower down but at Martha's end unsurfaced and leading up to a farm, which meant that there was no through traffic in the actual street and children played in clusters on the doorsteps and the pavements, and at the bottom of the steep hill was a busier road with an infrequent bus and some shops and a pastoral canal and open country; that the tiny back garden with its outside lavatory and coal bunker extended on the outer side of the fence into fields where cows came closer and closer as the day wore on till they munched the tea-towels or mats or jeans that had been thrown over the fence to dry; that the village had once been grouped round a mill that had recently closed down, taking the living heart out of the place; that her own immediate family and larger circle were what for brevity can be called a hippy community loosely grouped round a college of education though taking in other people too; look at this long vital list of words:

NOUNS

Home	*Body*	*Food*	*Outside*
FIRE	HEAD	WATER	STONES
WOOD	HAND	MUESLI	FIRE
COAL	FACE	RICE	WOOD
CLOCK	FINGER	BREAD	STICKS
WATCH	THUMB	MARMITE	STEPS
WINDOW	EYES	BEANS	LADDER

Chapter 7

Home	Body	Food	Outside
DOOR	NOSE	PEAS	TENT
STAIRS	MOUTH	BISCUIT	COW
BOOK	HAIR	APPLE	HORSE
PAPER	TEETH	SALT	SHEEP
PEN	CHIN	CHEESE	RABBIT
TELEPHONE	TOES	CAULIFLOWER	DOG
CIGARETTES	FEET	BANANA	DONKEY
PIPE	TONGUE	PEAR	CAT
MATCHES	BELLY-BUTTON	PEACH	FLOWER
TOBACCO	CHEST	CHOCOLATE	TREES
TIN	KNEES	SPAGHETTI	WATER
FLOOR	TUMMY	TEA	GRASS
MACHINE	TITS	MILK	LINE
(e.g. Hoover)	PENIS	FISH	(washing)
GLASSES	BUM	SPOON	DUCK
MUSIC	EAR	FORK	PARK
(i.e. TV, radio,	NECK	KNIFE	BRIDGE
etc.)	ARM	PLATE	
WORDS	BACK	MUG	

Home	Street	Sky	Clothes
IRON	HOUSE	BIRD	COAT
AXE	CHIMNEY	SKY	SHIRT
SAW	LIGHTS	SUN	VEST
WATER	SHOP	AEROPLANE	JERSEY
TABLE	MACHINE	FLY	SHOES
CHAIR	MAN	BUTTERFLY	SOCKS
MONEY	LADY	CLOUD	BOOTS
BRUSH	BABY	MOON	BUTTONS
COMB	CAR	RAIN	ZIP
MIRROR	VAN		DRESS
LETTER	TRUCK		ANORAK
STAMP	LORRY		TROUSERS
TOP (of pens)	CARAVAN		POCKET
WASP	BIKE		HAT
FISH	ENGINE		HOOD
	TRACTOR		BAG
	WATER		
	PUDDLE		

Toys	*Bed*	*Bath*	*Misc.* *Exclamations*
PAINT	NAPPY	TAP	OH DEAR
CRAYON	CREAM	TOWEL	NO
BOX	PINS	SOAP	BEEP BEEP
BALL	PANTS	FLANNEL	BANG
TEDDY	(at this time	WATER	PLEASE
SAND	she only wore	SHAMPOO	BOO
BUCKET	nappy and		WHAT'S THAT?
SWING	pants in bed)		WHO'S THAT?
BRICKS			HELLO
BUBBLES	POTTY		HIYA
BALLOON	BLANKET		OK
DOLL	BOTTLE		RIGHT
	COT		READY
	SHEET		TA
	TEAT		GOODBYE
			BYE BYE

Qualities		*Verbs & V. Phrases*	
MINE	MORE	SIT	OUT
WET	DIRTY	JUMP	DANCE
CLEAN	SHITTY	SLEEP	SHHH . . .
HURT	SHARP	KISS	CUDDLE
BURN	FUNNY	BITE	CRY
BUSY	NICE	FALL	PULL
EMPTY	ONE	PUSH	CARRY
TWO	MUSIC (almost	PICK (flowers)	SMELL (flowers)
GONE	adjective)	CAN'T FIND IT	I'LL DO IT
HOT	WARM	GO AWAY	GET IT
ANOTHER	STUCK	DON'T WANT IT	RIDE
ON (clothes)	UPSTAIRS	WASH	PEE
DOWNSTAIRS	AGAIN	PISS	SHIT
BROKEN		BACKWARDS	OPEN
		EMPTY	STICK (stamps)
		DRINK	EAT
		TICKLE	SWIM
		DROPPED IT	MEND IT

(Interesting that because of her life-style she had as yet no relation-ship words – neither familial nor hierarchical; she used people's names.)

All of these, of course, are words within her own experience, and rising entirely from it. Yet this was a rural village that had lost its working and living heart, and that had no 'cultural' amenities (no library, no cinema) apart from television sets – the kind of place teachers would say offers no experience and where a child is 'deprived' (as indeed adolescents often are). But a baby, and a really young child, needs very few 'instruments of growth' (to use a Peckham Centre phrase) that are not already within the average home and the immediate environment, and if he is allowed to use them he grows at an amazing pace.

What he *does* need, for at least a year and a quarter or a year and a half, is an Important Adult who calmly and delightedly, because she (or he) is confident, happy, and ever-growing in her own identity and her own place in the world, helps him build up on his. For some time already, *slowly* and at his own pace (if this has been appreciated) he has been weaning himself in many different ways; and now this weaning moves faster, still at his own pace. And now the adult begins to wean herself (or himself), till eventually their lives are separate but interweaving.

Perhaps it is factors like this – the confidence, the happiness, the constant growth and the respected identity of the child's Important Adult – that decides whether the young child is 'cul-turally deprived' or not (to use today's fashionable educational phrase). This has nothing whatever to do with what information schools 'put into' the child, but may have a great deal to do with what schools and society at large, directly or indirectly, do to the young child's Important Adult.

The first word Martha ever said was 'Bird'. When she was a baby, birds filled her with excitement and wonder. At three she was always trying to creep up and catch them.

The first word Emily said was 'Door'. She lived and played, as baby and toddler, in this village street, with front doors opening on to living rooms, where she could push every door open, and there to her delight was a family she knew, *living*! (Not necessarily always to the delight of the family. As she stood there, door wide open to the Lancashire wind, face radiant with discovery, trans-fixed – SHUT DOOR, LASS! the whole room roared.) Doors for me too as a child were always charged with magic, fear, trembling and delight.

There is a door in a picture book I have given Emily, but it's ornate, Georgian, at the top of an elegant flight of steps. There's a bird in the book too, but it's a gaudy parrot in a cage, not a bird strutting on the common, or clapping its wild way into the sky. Yet surely a plain door, showing an enticing glimpse of warm life inside, and a plain wild bird, would have been familiar to many more children, and would take excitement from their own experience. For a work of art or of education is made where the artist and the audience *meet*; each draws the other halfway, and in that meeting each remembers, each therefore imagines, and that is where the book, the play, the lesson, or whatever it may be, blazes into life.

So how can children who are not allowed to build on their own experience, not allowed, so to speak, to remember, ever imagine?

Words are true

Such a child, surrounded by books, has parents who are always reading books, too, and reading with great absorption. In fact sometimes the baby will have to pull the parent away from the parent's book towards the child's book, very much as sometimes the child will pull the mother away from the father, and towards himself (for by now the book *is* the child – Sam is inside this book; this book is about Sam; *read it, look at me, pay attention!*). In addition, the very fact that the parent is looking at his own book, means that a book is part of grown-upness, to be imitated and admired. In this family, for a child *not* to want to look at books would be odd, and seen perhaps as something to be worried or sad about.

As the child gets a little older, his books get a little more complicated, and the pictures are no longer just familiar objects, but familiar happenings; but still all that sensuous physical intimacy goes with the experience, and the same personal identification – 'Look, a park. You went to the park today, didn't you? And you fed the ducks too . . . .'

This mother will point to the word she is reading, or she will follow the words along the line with her finger; so that the child vaguely absorbs the shape and the length of familiar words that are important to him about familiar things that are important to him, spoken lovingly and laughingly and in safety; and he absorbs too – *still a baby* – the fact that English is read from left to right, and that pages are turned in a particular direction. And soon he will begin to 'read' the story aloud himself, imitating and reproducing what the adult read that filled him with such delight when he heard it – just as he imitated and reproduced his parent's language earlier when he couldn't say separate words but only the tune. Now the magic of the word is extending even more.

At the same time, in other ways, this child, exploring the exciting things adults can do, will string different observed ingredients of a situation together and then of his own volition add *the magic sound* that should transform this chaotic unperforming jumble into a satisfyingly functioning unity. Earlier the one-year-old will lay a sock on his foot, hoping it will somehow coalesce into a sock-with-a-foot-in-it. But a little girl of two may hold a pretend match to a gas fire, and when nothing happens remembers *the magic sound* and say POP – thinking 'Now, surely *now* it will work!' In another few years, this belief in the magic power of words, that began with the baby who summoned a powerful slave by a serendipitious combination of sound, will have been formalised into 'Abracadabra', and literature and mythology and theatre and conjuring tricks will come to this child from outside, joining up with his own imaginative exploring, and confirming him in his belief in the magicness of sounds. (Many adults have never moved out of this area of childhood, and they still string oddments together in this haphazard fashion, searching for the magic ingredient that will make everything coalesce and work; perhaps they never fully experienced their childhood, or perhaps they never had books, or perhaps the books that they had never used their own reality as a base from which to move forward.)

Just after Martha's second birthday Su and Dan came to London, and left her with me for the day. I listened to Su, talking to her.

'Martha, do you remember, I told you before ... In a little while now Dan and I are going to Swiss Cottage. You're not going. You're staying here with Leila and Harry. Only Dan and I are going. ...'

'Dick's going too.' (Not argument, but testing if she had it right.)

'Yes, Dick is going at the same time. But he's not going to Swiss Cottage with Dan and me. He's going to meet Wizzy, and he'll come back later. But not with us. He'll come back with Wizzy.'

'And Rollo!'

'Yes, Rollo'll come too. And later on they'll bring you to Dan and me at Swiss Cottage. In the van.'

'The red van? The red van's broken.'

'No, the red van isn't broken any more. It's mended now. Dan and I are going in the blue van to Swiss Cottage. And you and Dick and Wizzy and Rollo will come in the red van to Swiss Cottage. But that will be much later. After dinner.'

'Yes!' (Radiant smile.)

I listened to this, and thought it was ridiculous telling a two-year-old child all these complications.

When Su and Dan left, Martha didn't even go to the door to see them off – just called, 'See you later', and went on with what she was doing. Through the whole day, in a house she had never been left in before, all she showed of anxiety was to say, twice, 'I want Su.'

What struck me most, in a very odd way, was that everything happened exactly as she had been told. That Dick did go with them, but came back without them. That he didn't come back till much later, after dinner. That Wizzy and Rollo came back with him, and they came back in the red van. That they did have tea and a rest. And that later, Dick and Wizzy and Rollo and Martha went off in the red van to meet Su and Dan at Swiss Cottage. It seemed to me, conditioned not to explain all these details to a child of two and therefore used to the miasma of stumbling uncertainty and prevarication that surrounds dealings with a baby, absolutely remarkable the way events clicked in just as they had been recounted – almost as if I expected the *events* to be uncertain, and as if I felt the words, spoken the same over and over again, had in a magic way disciplined and taken charge of the events. It must seem like this to a child.

A child brought up like this not only talks and understands but has complete confidence in adults and in herself. Martha's vocabulary and sentence structure is, by our conditioning, which we mistakenly call expert knowledge, extraordinary. She had never heard of Swiss Cottage before. The first time she tried to repeat it, she tripped over it. The second time and every time after, she had it right. (This is the age – three years before entering school – when children are fascinated by words.) Before Su went, she gave Martha an apricot out of my jar. During the day Martha asked for another.

'I want a helicopter. Please.'

'You mean an apricot.'

'Yes. I want an apricot. Please.'

Christy, also age two, playing with an older brother, was caught up in a similar echoing of sound.

'Want elephant!' he demanded peremptorily.

'What elephant?'

'Elephant in cupboard.' (He tugged furiously at a stuck door.)

'There isn't an elephant in the cupboard!'

Christy triumphantly jerked open the door, revealing – a toy telephone. 'Elephant!'

Everything Martha told me on that day was true. I don't think it had ever before occurred to me – who enjoy and respect children – that I could rely for absolutely accurate information on everything a two-year-old told me. The only times I was doubtful was when I hadn't got her tune; but when I realised 'Feff' was a man called Seth, and that Rollo was a dog and that he belonged to someone who really was called Wizzy, my confidence in her never wavered.

Babies learn from birth to talk. They do it of their own accord. They don't have to go to school first, to learn phonetics or sentence structure. They learn in the cradle and the pram – first from their own free playful exploration, then from the important people round them, their own important people.

And if the child's 'important people' encourage and delight in the child, and if neither they nor society clamps down, then the child not only becomes fluent, but learns the self-organising power of words . . . the power that enables a child to predict and plan a future.

'*Dear Billy . . .*'

Such a child lives in a home that has time to spare, or at any rate gives time to its children, believing them very important, and has allowed him to spend hours, when he is only one, taking books out of shelves and putting them back, taking biscuit tins out of cupboards and putting them back, snuggling under chairs or tables – all those natural explorations that among so many other matters spontaneously discover size and shape (which will help him later to recognise letters and words) not academically but with his own physical identity. Soon, having explored first of his own volition, naturally growing, he will be playing games given him that deliberately build on this awareness and interest – posting boxes, stacking-beakers, jigsaws, or beakers and saucepans bought for adult use but freely lent to the child; for everything he does is watched with interest.

Or he is being lifted up to fit a *real* letter into a *real* letter box. For this is a home where letters arrive, friendly warm letters; and a home where people *write* letters, of their own choice, because they enjoy it, and because through letter-writing they keep in touch with friends and relatives. While this child is still a baby his podgy fist will be held over a pencil and helped to make a cross for a kiss, on a letter that magically goes out of the house; and magically a letter will come back with a kiss for him. A little while longer, and the kiss that was made for him will become a scrawled and incomprehensible picture that he makes himself, and magically again a picture will come back for him. And later still a message will be written at his dictation (and perhaps he will go out to post it – perhaps because *time* is given to children in his home he will wait to watch the postman open the box and will tell him about this letter), and a message, perhaps even a whole carefully-written page in an envelope bearing his own written name, will come magically back for him. So very early on he learns that words are first for showing him he is cherished, and then for moving towards other people who are also cherished by him, and by others; that sung, spoken, written, or read, words are for loving communication that is rooted in physical caressing, and that this satisfying expressiveness is something he can take part in.

I remember when Martha actually wrote her very first letter. It said

HARRY
MARTHA

in large flailing letters. What a powerful letter! 'Harry – you are there, and I am here! When will you come again to stay with us? Do you remember when you came before? Harry!' Power. Urgency. And a tremendous sense of magic. That letter was written because Dan was writing a letter to me, and then Su said she might write one to Harry; among her father and mother who were writing, this three-year-old took a pencil and wrote. It was such an exciting achievement that Su's letter was very brief: 'I was going to write you a letter, but after Martha's I feel inadequate!'

Years ago we used to write letters in my nursery school. I would sit down with a huge sheet of paper and a thick pencil and say 'Does anyone want to write a letter?' Then 'Who is it you want to write to?' And the child would say 'Mum' or 'Patrick' or 'Billy' – that was the guinea pig. So I would write for the child 'Dear Mum'. And then I would wait – and wait. And at the beginning I would think 'The child needs help'. So I would suggest things, adult things. I would say 'Perhaps you'd like to tell Mum what you made with the clay this morning?' I thought, you see, that words were for information. And the child would say 'No'. Everything I said was quite irrelevant. So I learned to wait. And eventually it came, with that exhausted but satisfied radiance you see on a mother's face after good childbirth. 'Dear Patrick, You are my friend.' 'Dear Billy, I will always look after you.' 'Dear Mummy, I love you very much.' These children knew what words set down on a page were for: they were emotional, they were about relationships, they were about identity. No-one had told them this academically. They had absorbed it from experience.

The child and the tigers

So this child begins to listen to stories. They may, as I said earlier, be stories quite specifically about him, made up solely *for* him *about* him, by his own adult – because the adults in a book-child's life have a background full of the rhythm and pace of hundreds of assimilated stories, and they use words easily, savouring them and savouring the construction of sentences and plots; they know books are about real people and are told by other real people, and they are not embarrassed within the warmth of their own family by their amateurishness or even conscious of it; and they encourage, and are intrigued by, the very personal identity and individual needs of each one of their children. For this family always has space and time.

Other times they may read printed stories. Sometimes these may be stories of everyday happenings, told realistically – the sort of things that have visibly happened to the child who is hearing the story, even though this story is a professional one and not made up personally for him, so that he turns to the adult with a smile of wondering complicity. They are familiar everyday experiences as far as this child is concerned, but they are shot through with illumination because the observation of children that impels them is exact and unsentimental, and because the language, though simple, is sharp, and the empathy is not only affectionate but serious. Both the writer of the story and the adult who reads it aloud roughly know the same children (writers will often get letters from such parents or grandparents saying 'How uncanny your stories are; they are so exactly about our three-year-old, I feel sure you must have met him somewhere!') and they roughly share the same attitude to them (this must be so, since otherwise the books would not stay in print; books only continue by being bought).

Sometimes instead the same real story about this three-year-old is told symbolically. And his growth and explorations, his developing independence and the fears, frustrations and rages, as well as the pride and satisfaction it brings, are presented as a journey from home, as they might well be in a dream. He wanders through a forest or a jungle, or along a river, where he meets tigers, or Wild Things, or trolls; half-playfully, rhythmically and ritualistically (for it is very important that this 'dangerous' part of the story most of all should have a shape that the child can quickly learn to control and participate in, with growing pleasure and predictableness) they pounce and try to destroy him. But he conquers them with his own growing competence, or maybe with the generous uncensorious help of older people in the family. And finally he goes back with new serenity to the affection of home – which is always represented by food . . . pancakes . . . juicy green grass . . . 'his supper that was waiting for him; and it was still hot'.

'The Three Little-Billy-goats Gruff', 'Little Black Sambo' and 'Where the Wild Things are', are all the same story – traditional, Victorian, or contemporary, an absolutely basic story of any human two to four year old. (I am deliberately saying this here, since recent social changes in England have completely disorientated 'Little Black Sambo' and got some people thinking it is the story of a black child living in Africa written by someone abysmally ignorant of facts.)

The child listening to the story *is* the Billy-goat Gruff – the *First* Billy-goat Gruff who could only get out of danger by throwing it on to his big brother, the *Second* Billy-goat Gruff who could only get out of danger by throwing it on to the next big brother, and the *biggest* Billy-goat Gruff of all who *can* manage and who isn't filled with anger at the cowardliness of the younger ones because he accepts that they are only little, and who capably and satisfyingly fights for them. The child listener is them all – the ones he is now and the ones he will grow into.

And the child listening to the story *is* Little Black Sambo. And he is also the tigers. He is the happy loved child, whose parents give him beautiful things, and also the fierce wicked tigers who want to tear him and these presents apart, who descend on his happiness from nowhere for no reason.

And the child listening is Max ... and also the Wild Things, making this tremendous rumpus, which Max learns to control, magically, and then sails calmly home; he is all these things ... both the 'good' and the 'bad', both the calm and the raging, both the smiled-at-by-Mummy-and-Daddy and the frowned-at-by-Mummy-and-Daddy, finally both the controller and the controlled. In the loving security of his nursery, sitting on a warm lap, with arms round him, he knows that all parts of him are accepted, that people know he will grow into maturity, and are not menaced by him.

Chapter 11

Frogs or pearls

When such a child is three, he maybe goes with his mother – even with his father sometimes, for his father has the sort of job that allows him to give time to his child – to a children's bookshop. For this child's family lives in a district that has a real dedicated children's bookshop in it – not a stationer's, or a tobacconist or a supermarket with a rack of paperbacks, nor a Woolworths, but a bookshop; and if they don't, then his mother or father will take him to a bookshop in a car or bus, because they know where bookshops are, they are used to them, and enjoy themselves and relax in them.

In the Children's Book Centre in Kensington, an expensive area of London, I often watch a father or mother looking at books with a child. The adult and the child together will look through a dozen or twenty easily, read the stories, talk about the pictures; and the child will run about, lift down other books, and bring them to his parent to be read and looked at. No-one will complain. That is what the shop is for. The staff are trained for this, and are delighted the child is taking such interest in the books. Two hours and twenty books later, the child and the parent may go out of the shop without even buying a book, because the child did not see one, or rather *experience* one, that was his own book. No-one will mind. They will come back another day, because they will both have enjoyed themselves, spend another two hours looking and reading and discussing, and perhaps this time the child will choose a book that *he* feels is his own. But whatever day the child goes out of that shop with a book, it will be his own book, chosen by him, experienced as *his book*.

Chapter II

Such a child will have his own bookshelf where his books are
recognised as his own private possessions, just as he has his own
bed, his own room, his own toys, his own pictures, his own chair;
his right to his personal identity is always stressed. There is space,
inside and outside his home, for exploring and, through exploring,
for growing, in tranquillity and at his own pace.

Yet as well as having tranquillity, he will take part in lively
outings to museums, galleries, festivals, theatres, picnics . . . and
will go on longer holidays to the country or the sea. The names
and the notices they see on the way will be read out, and talked
about, and fingered, and everything they see will be discussed or
touched. The young child will be expected to join in the talk, and
what he says will be listened to with respect and interest, and his
questions will be carefully answered, and his requests for new
outings, or repeated ones, will be welcomed and considered – for
his family has time and money and their life doesn't consist of
nothing but work or the terror of not having work; and besides,
going on these outings with their children comes naturally to
them, since it happened to them as children.

I was on a train some time ago, and in the same long carriage
was a young upper-middle-class mother and two boys. The three
of them discussed everything that was happening in very carrying
voices that came clearly to every passenger right down the
carriage, supremely self-confident about their place in the world.
After a wait at a station, the mother wondered aloud why they
were waiting, and the older boy said it was because they were
changing engines; he had heard it announced. After some brief
discussion they quickly rose and made their way to the window
which they opened, to watch the job being done, to comment on
it, to explain, to question. When it was finished, they came back
to their seats, where for the benefit of the younger child they read
every notice, loudly, and discussed them, the meaning of the
words, the reason for the notice. I found myself thinking that if
the accents had been working class, people would have been very
annoyed; as it was they were careful not to catch each other's eyes,
English-fashion. But what was happening was absolutely admir-
able, and very typical; all that was irritating was the loud egotism
that seemed to be blind to everyone else, the implicit assumption
that the world was theirs. There were several other families in the
carriage, and two or three of the fathers could easily have been

railwaymen themselves but no-one else's voice offered any contribution to a discussion that had in one sense become public, though in another it was very elitist indeed.

On these outings, such a child, without having to be from an arrogant class, nevertheless absorbs the fact that when his parents open their mouths to speak, complete strangers listen to their words with friendliness and respect. Yes, even policemen. It's like the fairytale – when their adults open their mouths, diamonds, pearls and rubies tumble out: a good powerful *magic*. Later on, perhaps only a year later on, when they start school, these children will discover this about their own words too, that they are jewels that delight people; whereas other children will find that only frogs and toads hop out of theirs.

Surviving the
Siamese cat

By the time this child starts state school at five, he will be almost able to read – not necessarily because he has been deliberately taught to read though that may also have been added, but because words – spoken, sung, read, written, – have from the beginning been intimately part of his personal life, and personal growth, personal magic, and personal power.

Indeed, if some years ago teachers hadn't practically ostracised children who came to school able to read, and their mothers who, teachers seemed to think, had been acting as pre-school pedagogues without training or a union card, I believe practically all children from such homes would be coming to school able to read – just as almost all children from all homes come to school able to walk and to speak, even though their parents are unqualified except that they habitually walk and talk themselves, and that they love and accept the child and are happy for him to imitate them in this, and the child loves and accepts them and is spontaneously eager to imitate them in this; and these are the greatest qualifications of all.

It seems to me ludicrous that we cannot welcome, into state schools, children who can already read. In itself it is an indictment of what passes as education. But it is also very short sighted. For *provided that the atmosphere is non-elitist and non-competitive*, such children can very easily help the others to read; but perhaps the proviso depends on our society itself being non-elitist and non-competitive, and we have a long way to go in achieving that.

I remember Martha, aged just two, fascinated by the exuberant place-changing dance of relative pronouns.

'This is *my* dinner,' she said, pointing 'And that's *your* dinner.'
'Yes,' I said, playing the game, and pointing too, but the opposite way to her. 'This is *my* dinner. And that's *your* dinner.'
'Yes!' she said, and laughed! '*My* dinner!' (a great joke to her) – '*Your* dinner.'

'Yes, *my* dinner.'

In a school or a university such a matter would be considered a very difficult intellectual concept; and believe me, it would be *made* difficult. Yet Martha came to it of her own accord, in her home, at the age of two . . . as do millions of other children.

It is necessary for a child to walk and talk, and joyous and rewarding for him to walk and talk, and he is spontaneously eager to do it, since the world most immediately around him is made up of walking and talking older people, whom he wants to accompany, run to, call to, talk to; he finds new delights when he begins to walk and talk, that make him stronger and more confident and more sure that life is exciting, and that lead to more walking and talking. For a smaller number of children the same happens with reading.

For such a child, even the dullest school readers imaginable, (which are very different from the books he has known previously which reproduced the rhythm and the tune, the words and the phrases, of the language he knew, and that shared jokes with him and his family) will not be able to completely make this child forget the joys of reading – though they may well make him apparently unable to read in school.

There are many things wrong with the pre-*Nippers* school reader (this term will be explained later), all of them stemming from the fact – which may come as a surprise to some parents – that they are not so much books or introductions to books, as tools of social control; their purpose is not so much to introduce the child to the delights of reading and writing and therefore all personal expression, as to train him for conformity and decorum (which is the opposite); not so much to open a gate for him, as to half-close it. (Robert Graves once wrote that myths and fairy-tales defend the *status quo*. So do school readers.) The child who has already moved forward creatively will find them retrograde, boring, frustrating, but his five years of creative experience may enable him to stand up to them.

I was once told at a lecture of a child who was reported for a long time by his teacher as being unable to read. 'Don't worry. Don't push him. He's simply a late developer.' The parents were used to books, and to reading, and they were astonished; but whenever the mother raised the point with the teacher, she was told 'Just don't worry. Don't push him. He's simply a late developer.' One morning, at breakfast-time, the child read out *The Times* leader. Dead silence. Then –

'But you can't read! Miss X says you can't read!'

'Of course I can read!' (weary scorn)

'Well, why don't you read at school?'

'Well, at school we only have *Janet and John*. Who wants to read *that*! It's so boring!'

I told this at another lecture, and the warden of a Teachers' Centre capped it with an almost identical experience with her child – also reported to the parents' bewilderment a non-reader. ('But don't worry – he's a late developer'.) One day when she came home, the boy told her 'There's been a very bad accident on the M1. Five people killed and thirteen people taken to hospital. Five cars all piled up. And four ambulances came, and two fire engines. I hope Daddy didn't drive home that way.' She assumed he had heard it on the radio – but he hadn't; then that his elder sister had heard it on the radio, and passed it on to him – but she hadn't; the radio hadn't been on. Then she picked up the evening paper to see if it had a picture, but it hadn't. It did have, however, a full-page news-story. The boy watched her bewildered face, and laughed.

'I *read* it.'

'But you can't read!'

'Of course I can!'

'Why don't you read at school then?'

'We only have that rotten *Janet and John*. I'm not reading *that*!' (This child incidentally was passionately interested in vehicles of all kinds as well as in his father – like many children.)

She and her husband went to the school, spent an embarrassing time telling the teacher the child really could read, and eventually solved the problem by making a donation of varied books to the school, so that their own child, as well as the other children, would have something he enjoyed reading.

These stilted graded readers not only sometimes stop the child reading the readers; sometimes they stop the child reading anything else, so that a great anxiety grows *not* to dare to read Book 3 before he has finished Book 2, and later even, *not* to dare to read a book that is not a school reader. This anxiety sometimes even spreads to stories of children's books that have nothing to do with school, so that I have heard a child say very nervously in a bookshop, 'Do I have to read all of these or can I go on to something else?'

Also they paralyse his writing. Two teachers at a remedial centre

both observed that a clever six-year-old, highly literate and orate, had in a peculiar way reverted to banality whenever he told them what he wrote in his NEWS at school.

On one occasion he was jumping up and down with excitement at the effect of the sun following a heavy shower. He was describing this event, which had clearly had a great effect on him, in a most interesting way, when one of the teachers said that he ought to put this in his News.

'I will,' said the child, 'I'll put Today ... I ... saw ... the sun ... come out ... it ... had ... been ... raining.'

This after a beautiful spontaneous description! The importance of this observation is that this peculiar stilted style is typical of children who write News, especially if they have begun to learn to write at the same time as they have begun to learn to read using graded readers. The teacher tends to reinforce the patterns used in Janet and John or what have you, always artificially simple and sometimes tediously repetitious. (I quote from a letter.)

And take a look, for lessons in 'acceptable behaviour', at pages like:

'Dolls are for girls,' says Susan.
'Kites are for boys,' says Peter.
'Kites are not for girls.'
(What a ludicrous conning – 'Little boys, little girls, don't do that.' They're doing it *now*, in front of you, daily. That's why you're saying 'Little boys, little girls, don't do that.')

Children of six or seven who have learnt both to be aware of themselves, and to express themselves verbally, often retain consciously a certain wistfulness, which is part of their sincerity and whole-heartedness. Richard Adams, age seven (I take this from the Leicestershire primary school broadsheet 1967, where contributors' spelling has been tidied up) writes:

'What I would like to do is to be a Geologist but the thing that stops me is school. Why I want to be one is because it has some interesting facts which you can find out on rocks which are called fossils where you can find out about Dinosaurs like the Ornitholestes, Allosaurus, Brachiosaurus which means arm Lizard. But the thing that stops me is school.' As school continues, the conflict for many children between what they really want to do, and what schooling demands of them, becomes unbearable, and they may agree to forget what they really want to do.

Our culture, man-made, tries to deal with everything by taking it out of its context. But when a one-year-old is feeding in his high chair – such a complicated piece of natural learning I shudder to think what schooling would make of it – he is just as likely to be listening to you singing while he concentrates hard on putting a lid on and off a feeding cup or a yoghurt carton, or savours with his hands the consistency of his porridge, as being interested in feeding; though if you do not forbid this particular exploration, concentration, and self-chosen development of skill, he opens his mouth abstractedly and swallows the food. If instead you say 'This is the time for *eating*, and this high chair is the place where you *eat*', he won't eat at all; or if he does, he will do it under protest and strain, with his own impetus taken away from him, and his own self-confidence in developing skills already eroded. (Similarly, an older child while listening to a story may be talking to his teddy or into a toy telephone, or playing with a train, or even looking at another book. With a pathetic need to be appreciated (because as mothers we have had to surrender or suspend our own identity and can only exist by reflection) we say 'Are you listening? I'm not going to go on if you're not listening.' But if, instead, we paused and said conspiratorially 'and then?' the child would show he was listening by telling the next bit of the story.)

Often in the course of a meal, in a period when he is concentrating on some manipulative toy while eating and has to be fed, Kit (age fourteen months) will bend forward for a crooning cuddle, as if a quick renewal of the warm, physical relationship that went with the breast is still pleasant and useful. Eventually you both decide the meal is finished and lift him down, and five minutes later this baby who seemed lately to have thrown over all interest in tidily spoon-feeding himself in favour of putting holed shapes over a stick is crouched over a low table concentratedly putting a conker on his spoon and carrying it carefully to his mouth, over and over again. The baby has growth *inside* him. You can only help his own growth by seeing what he is doing from his angle and respecting it, or you can hinder his growth.

Teachers, who are obedient defenders of our culture, take reading out of its context, and then look around busily to supply a 'motivation' which they have noticed – shaking their heads sadly – is missing; or they will put together in a great artificial 'project' the things the system has just arrogantly and brutally forced apart – rather (picking up one from a myriad current examples) as we take wheat-germ or bran out of food, and sell it back separately. And only the child who is already secure enough in *the basis* for reading or writing survives this.

For even the most boring, the most lifeless, the most rigid, the most brain-washing, the most monosyllabic readers cannot entirely take from such a child *what has been built up for five years and is fused with his growth*, the belief in himself, and the belief that books are his birthright – even though they may knock it back a little, or force him in secret scorn to conceal his private skill, stoically forget his longings, and put away for a while the passionate loving rhythm with which he once wrote and read.

And besides, although the family in the orthodox reader cannot exist at all – there is no family so griefless, angerless, humourless, or so utterly devoid of conflict as the family in the orthodox reader – it is recognisable in externals . . . the detached house, the clematis round the door, the roses and chrysanthemums, father at leisure with the lawn-mower (or going to the office with the brief case), the large dog and the aristocratic cat, the tidy organised family consisting only of one father, one mother, one son, one daughter, the polite conversation at the damask-covered breakfast table where obviously no-one clocks on, the regal gesture of the mother pouring the tea with gracefully turned wrist and handing it graciously to father, both seated. (Compare with the vast number of mothers who are always standing up to pour the tea, and who line up the mugs for their large families as if they are in a works canteen, and slosh the tea in an unending cataract backwards and forwards, filling the mugs in bulk almost incidentally . . . and with the families who never in their lives sit down to breakfast.) These at least bear a waxworks resemblance in *some* of

49

the details to his own family, which he therefore subconsciously realises is the accepted family. He is *still* able – if he wishes – to be in this uneasy uncomfortable book.

And his membership is confirmed by the fact that his head or his teacher talks much like his mother does, using the same words, phrases and tune; that she supervises him in much the same way as his mother does, and has the same expectations; that if she goes to tea with any parent, she will go to tea with his; that if a parent comes to school to discuss matters with a teacher or a head and is listened to with respect, interest and friendship, it will be *his* parent – and that when he writes his 'news' or dictates something for his teacher to write down, it is something his teacher is happy to hear. (Even if, to his bewilderment, she laughs, it remains affectionate 'membership' laughter.)

So he can still, with the help of his parents, insist on his own identity and the right to use reading and writing, which are this child's accepted heritage, to confirm and enrich this personal identity – even when as sometimes happens, even in a modern primary school, even with a 'book-child' – the thing that stops him is school. The whole person and the reader may be knocked back, but survives.

Factory babies

No-one looking at most future mothers – who have in any case had little nutritious food, or rest, or space to explore or relax in, or time to spare – sitting on the rows of straight-backed seats in the ante-natal clinic where they are regularly surrounded by reminders of catastrophe and evidence of touchy staff hierarchies, afraid to put a foot wrong or speak out of turn, waiting literally for hours for their name to be called from an impersonal pile of cards, sometimes with another child they've had to bring with them whom somehow they must keep quiet, still, and frustrated for these same hours on end, would claim this periodic experience gives the mother a sense of glowing and exciting well-being. No-one, listening to young mothers recently home from hospital, where they had been given drugs (even when they'd asked not to be given them) and forceps deliveries and caesarians and inductions, could claim they got exhilarating self-confidence from their co-operation at birth with their baby, or a proud delight in the capability, strength, tenderness, and achievement of their own body that would last through this baby's childhood.

They may not even have got a fully-developed baby, for it is certainly possible for induction to result in what is really a premature birth (though not declared as such). Do doctors give any thought to this, when they harness technological enthusiasm to convenience? Isn't it relevant to our surveys on children's reading ability that working-class children who are born from mothers who have often had mediocre food and sometimes depressing conditions in pregnancy, are also more likely than middle-class babies to be forced into the world before their senses and abilities are fully developed? (Middle-class mothers are informed about these matters. They read about them. Above all, they can argue – and with an 'educated' accent, which is more likely to be listened to.)

Following growing indignation among verbally-fluent mothers about induction, the Department of Health prepared a report (not published as I write, but featured in the *Sunday Times* 7 December 1975, very much a 'book-mother's' paper) in which they grant that 'Advantage may have been taken of . . . induction to reduce workloads during holiday periods', but add that 'there may be a case for more rather than less induction.' The report says, tongue in cheek, that visits by Health Department officials to hospitals where inductions were taking place revealed no evidence to substantiate claims that use of induction had led to 'a sausage machine hospital environment'; indeed, 'most clinicians we spoke to viewed the use of induction as a means to "improve the quality of the product" '. (Language was used in the same deliberately dehumanizing way in the Nazi concentration camps.) In the same feature is a report that the present work-to-rule by junior doctors has led to the speeding up of births in at least one hospital, Ashton-under-Lyne General, so that babies could be born between 9 am and 5 pm while junior doctors were still on duty.

Even when the baby is born with all his faculties ready for birth, the majority of mothers and babies have already had taken from them, by a system of experts, any belief in their own natural, healthy, competent and satisfying partnership. And how can they continue an intertwining relationship when the baby is handed to them only as a cleaned-up tightly-wrapped cocoon, a rigid monument to respectability, who seems never to have any connection with the outside of the mother's body, let alone the inside? With sensual pleasure and spontaneity completely inhibited, the baby seems to be only a monstrously demanding mouth, filling the mother with anxiety. There is no creative communication.

Within the next few days, this baby's senses are likely to be arrested further. In a calm relaxed environment a baby gets used to his new world at his own pace, exploring it slowly and gently. But here in a hospital with its clatter, its harsh light, its lack of gentle intimacy, its frustrations, its telephones, and its tense comings and goings, the baby is forced to defend himself, to pull his senses back, to shrink from the world. An American researcher, struck by the realisation that all our 'norms' of babies' development were based on hospital births, once studied babies in calmer, more relaxed, more private surroundings and discovered that their senses and abilities – their eye focusing, for instance – developed much faster than this 'norm'. That 'the norm', in fact, was telling us not what babies did, but what we did to babies.

Explorers keep out

'Don't talk to me about bloody neighbours! I'd like to get a bloody machine-gun and blow their bloody heads off! Woman upstairs, she says to me at *half-past three*, "Why don't you keep your children quiet!" she says to me. She says "My daughter works at night and she has to sleep in the day." I said "You tell your bloody daughter to get a bloody job in the bloody day same as everyone else, and sleep in the bloody nights!" '

This was a woman on my bus this morning coming back from Brixton, talking furiously at the top of her voice. Minutes later, she had got most of it off her chest, and was saying, still for everyone to hear, and still as a manifesto stating her identity, 'I used to be soft and nice, but where's it got me? Soft and nice. Now I'm tough like the bloody rest.' And finally, staggering off with her load of shopping and declaring an armistice 'Well, I'll go and sit down now and forget my troubles.'

Suppose a baby is brought from a clattering clinical hospital ward to a Council flat or house, which is produced as cheaply as possible with walls that are not much better than cardboard, or to an old tenement house lived in by several different families, or to one of those identical little villas with tiny gardens in a long, long terrace, where the passer-by can hear from the pavement when an inside lavatory is flushed. Any 'noise' from this baby, at any time of the day or night, is a threat – people will complain. How can this baby express himself? How can he playfully explore his own sounds?

Or maybe his father has to get up at 4 am and needs what sleep he can get; maybe both his father and mother go out to work, and *both* need to sleep at night before his mother takes him off to the day nursery, so his mother can't even face dragging herself out of bed to quiet him for father's sake; sometimes little Big Sister will be his nurse, and will have had to give up her own childhood for him, and the repressed anger that flames in her will not help anyone; but they have no other kind of help. Maybe his father works nights and has to sleep in the daytime; so the baby cannot even make sounds during the day.

Or maybe his parents hear his cry only as noise, not as communication, simply because their own parents never listened to them; they have never been on the crying side of *successful* communication themselves when they were babies, and this makes it very difficult to set it going now from the parent side. It is not only that one does not know how to; knowledge or understanding could, if need be, be gained from books – except, of course, that this family is not used to books, and hasn't the time now to learn in this way; but it's also that there has been a definite taboo in the family background, because of the family circumstances, against this communication, and the stone wall made up of old rejections and hurts and fears will now have to be climbed over by deliberate resolve, however painful and frightening and memory-reviving this is going to be. It's not surprising if they don't make this resolve, but prefer to believe babies' cries mean nothing, except annoyance, and must be resisted as their own were.

Sometimes, even so, the baby's crying does make the mother want to listen and understand, even though she never had this herself, even though circumstances make understanding one's baby almost impossible, but the conning advertising of the consumer society that tells her that if she uses the 'right' nappies . . . or antiseptic . . . or baby cream . . . the baby will stop crying and will love her, or the clinics of the welfare society that expect her and her baby to conform to the pattern they hand out prevent the two of them from discovering this mutual understanding, and instead confirm her failure and fill her with despair and anger.

For all these reasons, and others, 'Shut up' may be the first phrase that will be *deliberately* directed to this baby. So his days are very silent – that is to say, he does not experience the loving, lingering, time-ignoring words that were deliberately handed to the other child, inviting response.

Yet though he participates in very little conversation, or personal sound exploration, *noise* he has plenty of, noise and disturbance. The noise of people shouting, of traffic, of bulldozers and demolition gangs. The disturbance from other people who share the house, or his room or his bed, and get up and go to bed at different hours. (And this will continue throughout his life – day nursery period, school period, factory period: traffic, bulldozers, loudspeakers, machines, will so batter him down that he learns to communicate in shouted monosyllables. And when he is frightened or made uneasy by the quiet of the countryside, people who have had a more serene life will put it down to a sad lack of aesthetic sense.)

But that slow, gentle, sensuous and physical building up of his own identity with words and caresses is quite unknown to him. If as a baby his attempts at communication, which may be crying or squealing, continue, despite shouts or slaps, he is gagged with a dummy. He has to be, because he is in a situation where there isn't the time or the space for exploring communication. (He is already in the situation that will meet him again in school – 'Stop talking!' 'Be quiet!' Even a placard facing him in the library, saying SILENCE! And unlike the other child, he won't have built up the self-regard to weather it.)

A child's speech – and his writing and reading, and his thinking – are based on a baby's playful babbling. If a baby's babbling – playful exploration of sound – is so important, anything that prohibits, discourages, even fails to encourage it, is hostile to the baby's development, and anti-human. (Surely for years boys have taken up science at school more readily than girls because when younger they are expected to *babble* – or dabble – in it. They make stink bombs, they play with water and mud, they carry out – and are encouraged to carry out – numerous purely playful activities that are connected with science and exploration and finding out. By the time they come to science – the formal school subject – it is an old friend. But to a girl, most girls, it is something alien; they have to act against past prohibitions.) With different attitudes, different things may happen. One of Martha's early words was 'scriver' – screwdriver. Dan at the time was doing some electrical work around the house; she followed him round admiringly, and he gave her a screwdriver and wall-plug to play with; for a long time this combination was her favourite toy. One day, plug in one hand, she climbed up the almost perpendicular stairs, bringing both feet together on each step as she went up, for she was only a year and ten months, to ask Dan 'Where's my scriver?' Dan didn't have it, but Harry, up there too, had a penknife that had a screwdriver incorporated in it, and as he had seen the way Martha was brought up, and the responsible and competent way she behaved in consequence, he opened it at the screwdriver and gave it to her, saying very seriously, 'But be careful. This can hurt you.' 'Yes', she agreed, equally seriously. And she then proceeded to go back down the steep stair, backwards on all fours which was the only way she could manage, the plug clutched in one fist, the screwdriver-penknife in the other, and reached the bottom unhurt – Dan and Su never doubted it. At the bottom she stood up, and happily got busy with her plug and 'scriver' exploring in play its possibilities.

Gwen Chester once wrote of an upper-class baby whose Nanny was very silent. The child in consequence not only acquired very little speech, but in consequence of that found it very difficult to express, and therefore to control, anger. For only what is *expressed*, whether vocally or silently, can be seen, understood, controlled. The vast majority of our children do not have Nannies but have the heavy weight of an unaccepting, unloving, and uncommunicating society; and no adult joins in conversational games with them, tossing ideas, conceptions, and opinions, backwards and forwards like a ball.

Such a child has no space for exploring inside, no room of his own. How can a baby grow to his full capacity – how can he even *aim* – if he has no space (friendly space, that is still near his mother, and still dotted with helpful and interesting objects)? As I watched Kit grow *in babyhood*, I understood the perceptive depth of the phrase 'covering ground'. Kit, the baby, developed so much because he had space; and because he had space his muscles developed, and because they developed his aim and his reach was further, his movement larger and freer. As a baby grows – sits up, stands, reaches, walks with mother, walks away from mother – his new powers call out further new powers, and he covers new ground both literally and metaphorically.

But with the majority of our children, the most important room, the kitchen, which in a book-child's house is full of warm, loving, building-up smells, and where a child can linger, imitate adult skills, curiously taste different flavours, or sit under the table in

security and private quiet, watching the busy adult world, is often –
if he lives in a council flat – a tiny kitchenette where his harassed
mother even when alone scarcely has room to turn round; or it's
the main room of a tenement flat, dominated by the stove on
which there is always something boiling, so that the desperate
trapped mother keeps the child (no longer a baby) in a cot with
the sides up, or strapped in a pram or a high chair, unable to move,
unable to speak, and scarcely spoken to. Is a deeply depressed, or
a harassed, mother likely to hold conversations with her child?
(I know very well that in our present English society, many
mothers at home with their babies are isolated, depressed and
exhausted. But those with verbal fluency and some books in the
background at least know the baby has certain needs and that
words are one; and they will provide it, even though sometimes
it may be with a desperate obsessiveness that serves to bolster
their own disintegrating identity.)

Perhaps as soon as she can, to save her own sanity, she will put
him in a day nursery or with a minder. Since the kind of job she
can take (unlike the job the mother of the 'book-child' might take)
is almost bound to have long hours, he will stay there for a twelve-
hour day or not much less and their journey there and back,
almost the only chance they have of getting to know each other,
will be harassed and in darkness; and this may start from the time
he is only a month old or less (the time when Kit's mother was
first beginning to be aware of his rhythm, and he was beginning
to form trust, and communication was on the verge of beginning).

Day nurseries have long waiting lists; yet at the same time,
their main purpose is to act as refugees for the baby victims of
crisis. The atmosphere around them is one of almost permanently
frustrated urgency, and the staff, to protect themselves (all the
more so if they are conscientious or warm-hearted people) have
become resigned. They take babies 'at risk', babies who might
otherwise be assaulted, or else put into permanent care. However
good the matron, their vibrations are of tension just held at bay –
very like a hospital; and indeed their staff have traditionally been
hospital-trained.

They rarely, perhaps never, have enough or adequate staff, and
never will till all people who look after children are recognised by
our society as being important (and then, probably, their job will
change). As it is, many of the 'adults' who will look after this baby

are not only just out of school themselves, but are trainees who will move on after a few months and be replaced by others.

The older ones, more experienced, responsible and dedicated, have learnt early on to inhibit their response to the babies, not only because of their clinical training but also because they are so understaffed. 'A baby's cry is like a telephone bell. It's urgent – you want to answer it. But how can you, here? You have to steel yourself to ignore it,' said an excellent matron to me, who would have preferred it to be otherwise.

So learning mutual satisfying communication (and reading is a later development of this) is quite impossible for this baby. And the searching intense look on the face of the baby like Kit who naturally learns who is familiar and who is strange – which sets going not only the process of trust and relaxed growth but also the process of memory, on which is built so much of the baby's growth – perhaps never develops with this child, who has no constancy close to him to learn to recognise. Certainly when you go into a day nursery – where often even very young babies *being fed* are not held in someone's arms – the expression on babies' faces is apathy, a sort of emotional wariness, a withdrawal. At the beginning of his life, this child is already depressed; and it isn't a transitory state.

The day-nursery building is likely to be subject to local authority economies; when cracks in the ceiling are painted over, perhaps *only* the crack is painted over. This lack of cherishing affects the staff, and it affects the mothers if they ever stay long enough to see; the brushing-aside of their worth as persons colours their attitude to themselves, and affects the way they see the baby. It affects the baby too, in that this baby is *not* going to be held in someone's arms and taken round the room to look at attractive things that hang from the ceiling or are fastened to the wall, and to listen to gentle talk about them. Equipment, particularly books, are very scarce, and are certainly not deliberately chosen to follow, as well as to promote, this one child's development. In any case no-one would be available to play with him, or to show him books if they had any. He'll be lucky if any adult is available to talk to him, let alone to read to him.

He will probably spend all the ten to twelve hours of his nursery day with babies of his own age, even though we'd discovered at the end of the last war that this war nursery practice stultified a child's development, most particularly the development of speech. (Conservative training, inadequate staffing, and a building which is often an old house with a staircase – very stimulating and enfolding for a nursery school, but nerve-wracking for a current day nursery – help to prolong this old practice of age-grouping.) He might though be very lucky, and have a day nursery in his district where they have introduced family-grouping instead of age-grouping. If he can get into it, he may be able to hear a four-year-old talking (though this may, of course, be a four-year-old whose speech had been stultified). In those twelve hours, repeated for years before he starts school and is expected to be eager to read, he will never experience a one-to-one relationship with an adult.

It is appalling that though Dr René Spitz, Dr Bakwin and others discovered years ago that lack of physical caressing, of human communication, actually kills babies, we continue in 1975 to rear babies in conditions that, however conscientious the matron and staff may be, are in their essence near-lethal, so that though these luckier babies are not actually dying they are only half-living, growing up resigned, depressed, uncommunicative, lifeless (we call them 'unintelligent') or, if they have enough life left, are driven by hate, anger, or an insistence on attention (we call them 'tearaways' or 'delinquents').

If his mother is not so obedient and conformist, maybe the baby goes to a 'minder' instead. In one sense, this is a much better potential situation: he is in a private home, a small house, which is more child-size and more familiar to him, real activities go on around him, and the minder remains reliably the same, day after day. Perhaps his senses will begin to reach out more naturally. And indeed, a good minder, who perhaps takes only one baby in addition to her own family, can be an ideal mother-substitute, warm, personal, and responsible. But the more usual child-minder, who takes several children, rarely knows anything about babies' and children's needs, her facilities are far less than the limited ones of the day nursery, and she is often extremely repressive. Some local authorities like my own, Lambeth, thankfully moving away from the wholly hostile attitude to minders, now try to tempt them out of hiding (perhaps also out of individuality?) by offering training, state-paid salaries, useful facilities; and Save the Children Fund, in the same district, employ a social worker to help minders as well as mothers; but even so I have seen children at minders' scarcely moving all day, any still-flickering initiative or exploration instantly quelled. It is difficult to weigh up which is better – the closely concentrated repression and squalor a child gets from many minders, or the impersonal emotional blankness and clinical routine he will get in a day nursery.

In any case, both day nurseries *and* the usual minders have been invented to hold off catastrophe. They were not intended to be warm creative growing-places, deliberately and thoughtfully chosen by a mother, for a child who has shown he is old enough to want to move outside the home. The child is taken and brought back in haste, anxiety and frustration; there is no sharing of the day's experiences or of the child's doings. Often both journeys are in darkness. How can anyone pretend this situation is anything like that of the baby Kit's, or of an older 'book-child' going to a nursery school or play-group; and how can the communication of loving and playful touch, loving and playful words, loving and playful books, emerge from this emotional, intellectual, and sensuous privation?

If we wanted to help children to talk and read, the mother's isolated social situation, precarious financial situation, her perpetual exhaustion, and her belief – handed her by society, including the hierarchy of the teaching profession – that associates of babies and very young children are inferior, dull-witted adults, are the first things we would resolve to change. For surely a lively, loving, happy, and creative mother is the foremost developer of language.

There may be a balcony to this baby's flat, but the door to it is invariably locked, because it never occurred to the architect – or if it did occur to him the Council didn't want to spend the necessary money – that a balcony where a small child plays must be made safe, especially if the flat is several storeys up. (Yet how odd that the people on the Council – and the architect – live in quite a different kind of place. They weren't sent to live with small children in a flat on the twelfth or fifteenth floor. They don't spend several years there being told by 'experts' it was nonsensical to ascribe their anxiety and loneliness, or their children's isolation and withdrawal or delinquency, to the height in mid-air. They didn't after many years hear the same, or similar, experts announce that they had discovered high flats were bad for people. They didn't then have to continue to live in them.)

Outside, this child has nowhere to play either. Only concrete paths, many storeys down – if the mother did leave the child alone there it would be a half-admission to herself that she was being forced to want to abandon the child and that might well terrify her as much as the objective danger. At the end of the concrete paths are the streets with traffic roaring by. If anywhere on the council estate there is a patch of grass, it is almost bound to be forbidden.

In 1975, children in Lambeth, South London, asked to set down what they thought about the places they played in, and assured that what they said, wrote, or drew would have power to change matters, wrote:

> We are bullied about we can only play in the playground and even then we are chucked out so we have hardly no space to play. We go in the swings and the Big boys push us out again go and play in the grass they say so we go. We go in the grass then what do you hear get out get out get out. So we have to go on the streets the caretaker especially watches us.

> Go away before I phone the police. Go and play. Go away and don't come back. Get away from my car now get. Go were you live. O my ball.
> [These are captions on pictures of her street.]

> There is no where to play. If there is you can not play there the playground is too small. The boys don't let you in the playground. All the SPACE is used up. Not where to play for the children of W. Estate. But I like where I live even that it is small.

> Come here. Stop that. They won't let me play here. Leave off. I have only two rooms to play in. Shut up. I have lots of trouble round here. Go away.
> [More captions.]

The younger ones knew they needed to play near home. Eight-year-olds played in the street outside their homes, even though the common was only a minute away. (Most public open spaces had 'dangerous roads to cross', and the children said 'drunks hang about in them'.) Any grass their flats offered was immediately outside the ground-floor flats where the housing authorities had placed old people, without any buffer area in front of their windows and doors; and as play-space was so short, crowds of anonymous children came from other estates, terrorising the old people at first unintentionally, later, because it was the only excitement, probably intentionally. And any official tarmac playground (which adults considered 'the safe place') children considered the unsafe place. 'It's dangerous with broken glass', they said. 'Big boys come round and beat you up and kick your balls.' 'They carry nails to stick in you and put lighted matches against your face.'

Instead the children explore empty old houses, climb up garages and have races on the roof ('The dads run after us and chase us off. That's what we like'), play hide and seek round the flat corridors, go up to the top floor in the lift ('and a lady comes out with some wood and then we run down three floors'), climb their 'Mount Everest' (which turns out to be a mound of rubble which backs an empty building), or 'go up the Vicar's Hosepipe' (which is an area near the Vicar's house where they can walk along the wall and count on the vicar getting out a hosepipe to drive them off).

But the place they really love is the dump, waste-ground covered in weeds. They find things there, like 'snails in tin cans'. This is their countryside, the place they long for when they write about the way they'd like Lambeth to be, which always has beautiful flowers and 'baby deers born every year', and ponds full of fish and ducks and seals and dolphins and crocodiles. But they are not supposed to play there.

Just as one of the first phrases this child hears is 'Shut up', so one of the first phrases he sees written is 'Keep out'. He might, in fact, learn to read on this. But his teachers will not allow this because they will pretend most life is quite different from reality, and that everyone is saying 'Come in!' when in fact they are saying 'Keep out!'

Access to lions

When they had all eaten their sandwiches and drunk their orange squash, Jimmy rushed for the sand-pit. He took off his socks and shoes, and threw them to Gloria, who said nothing, but merely picked them up and put them in the pushchair. Then he scrabbled in the cool sand with his bare toes, and cheekily laughed at her, and she laughed back. Soon he was working very seriously, making a railway-line in the sand, for a piece of wood that he had found to puff and hoot along. He crawled through the sand on all fours, making his line. Once he accidentally dribbled from his mouth, and looked with interest at the little glass beads of wet that winked and wobbled on the sand; then he went back to his work again. . . .

Only Gloria wasn't playing. She looked at Jimmy in the sand-pit. He was very busy, very absorbed. She hesitated a moment, then stood up, and sauntered over to the big slide in a very grown-up, casual way. She gave one more glance at Jimmy. Then suddenly she dropped her grown-up air, dashed up the stairs as quickly as she could, and came streaming down the slide, free as the wind for two seconds. She shouted out loud for joy. She got to the bottom and stood up again in one movement, and she was just going to run round to the steps for another go, when Jimmy raised his head from the sand. He did not see her where he expected to, and turned round slowly to find her. She could have waved to him, and had her second slide; Jimmy would not

have minded; but instead she instantly put on her grown-up
air and walked back to him:

'Here I am, Jimmy. Did you think I had gone?'

A child like 'Jimmy' cannot wander out himself to explore, and
play. Unlike the first child he has no place outside his home
where he can wander, become absorbed, stretch himself of his
own accord physically and imaginatively – and still be safe and
unharassed.

If there is any park or playground in the district at all – and
there may not be – he is going to have to be taken there, when
someone has time to take him, and specifically *wants* to take him,
and makes a decision to do all the small things that go, in this
situation, with taking this young child out. To take him just the
other side of the main road, where maybe the only park is, in-
volves as much planning and side-action and nervous energy as
the other child's family spend on a far larger-scale expedition
(which incidentally will enrich the mother herself far more); and
precisely because she feels he *ought* to be able to go there on his
own, the mother can't help but mix irritation and frustration and
reluctance into the outing (which is so small-scale that it is
scarcely more than the play and picnic in his own garden that the
book-child has with his friends, daily, without any arrangement
at all), and this spills over on to the child, training him to feel his
need for exploration is bad, that there is something dangerous in
him, some natural force that he can do nothing about except
stifle, since it causes anger.

Sometimes little Big Sister will take him instead; and even
sadder frustration is involved then. The playgrounds that state
the age of the child who can use them, and the official gorgons
who chase little Big Sister away (with the little one) because
she is too old – too old to be allowed to take the younger one
in, too old to sit on the neighbouring swing herself and snatch
just a little childlike pleasure too while he swings up and
down. . . .

(Sometimes he doesn't even do better in this if his mother
takes him. At a paddling pool on the common, I have seen a
mother take off her shoes and stockings in order to take her baby
into the water – and be ordered out by the attendant for being too
old. The book-mother doesn't spend so much of her life in

confrontation with petty officials; and when she does, she at least feels their equal.)

The passage above, about Jimmy, is from a children's book of mine, *My Dog Sunday* (Hamish Hamilton, 1968), about a family with four children, where I describe such a relationship between sister and toddler. The toddler has been taken to the park, by his other sister and brother (who carried him on his back, a long and tiring way), while thirteen-year-old Big Sister Gloria finished scrubbing the floor, and then took the washing to the laundrette in the push-chair, meeting them after that in the park.

Little Big Sister, forced beyond her years in a specific way a child from a book home is not forced, and frustrated and separated from her own identity in a specific way that a book-child is not (I put it like this, for I recognise that in different ways all children, boys as well as girls, may be pressurised and distorted), is going to have to wrap into her mothering a lot of anger, self-assertiveness, and a need to be taken notice of *through* the baby that will hamper that baby's exploration even when the environment doesn't (and the more she carries out this mother role uncomplainingly, the more she will have to hamper him, for her own survival). When she becomes an actual mother, she will already have been trained to be both capable and hampering; I deliberately use 'trained' rather than 'educated', because education would have enriched not impoverished her.

So this baby is barred from the exploration that is open to the other child. A little later on, the basic need for physical skills that are a natural part of a child's growth, and that the other child in his garden or on his outing or on his expensively designed apparatus develops with adult approval (and that are one way of expressing self-esteem and communication with the world, just as words are another way), will set him swinging on bus shelter rails, hanging from London tube straps, jumping off escalator steps, running down the up escalator, climbing trees in the park or the surburban street, and he will be walloped or treated as a 'delin-quent'.

Some years ago I took five Sheffield children ranging in age from two to nine, to the West End of London. They had never been in London before, and they were wildly excited. I took them to Trafalgar Square. We got there by tube. I had expected the train doors to fascinate them, but hadn't also realised that straphanging – or rather strap-*swinging* through the jungle of an almost empty train – was such a spontaneous and exhilarating exercise for children cooped up in a condemned house in a slum!

I showed them Nelson and the Lions, and answered the instant question in their eyes with 'Sure. Why not. Everyone climbs on them.' I wandered round the square alone, sat down, looked at a newspaper. When I looked up again, *they were standing in the square, grouped round a policeman, who was writing down their names in a notebook.*

I got to my feet, and rushed across. The policeman was clearly embarrassed. 'I'm sorry, Madam. I had no idea they were with you.'

'But why were you taking their names! What had they done!'

'They were sitting on the lions.'

'I *told* them they could sit on the lions! *All* the children sit on the lions! Every week-end you can come here and find dozens of children *swarming* over the lions!'

'I thought they might endanger themselves, Madam. . . .'

Seething, I took them down to the river. There was no time to take them on a river-trip; I had to return them to catch a train. So I did the next best thing. I showed them the boats and then suggested that they take some leaflets of the various boat-trips that we could read and talk about on the way back.

Again, almost immediately it seemed, they were tearing along the embankment with an irate official in pursuit. What was the matter? 'They took some leaflets!'

'But the leaflets were there to be taken, weren't they? Weren't they stacked in those piles on the wall *to be taken*!' The official shuffled a bit, muttering. 'I *sent* them to take some leaflets!' I said, in a desperate rage.

This official didn't even say 'I'm sorry, Madam', however wildly I pushed up my accent. He stumped away, swearing.

I must say, the kids who had been shaken by the policeman were quite cheerful about the boatman. They were used to it; they expected it. They had believed me when I first said they could explore, but I had been proved wrong; they bore me no grudge.

Children with the right accents, the right modulations, the right gestures, could have sat on those lions and picked up those leaflets unmolested – and always did – even though they would not have had anything like the same urgent need for it.

'Hurry up' and 'Don't touch'

A child I talked to in an East End of London school remarked to me in a matter-of-fact tone, 'My Mum says when you've got ten children, you can't go nowhere.' And indeed how can they, with all the fares and the admission prices and the cost of refreshments for twelve? In that same primary school, the only children who ever did go out were the lucky ones whose father had a job that involved a van, which he could bring home, and did, though he probably wasn't supposed to; and on Sundays – probably breaking regulations – the whole family plus aunts, nephews, friends, and Nan, numbering sixteen or so, would pile into the van and go to Southend for the day. Is the new high price of petrol going to take away from such a child these outings he so rarely has?

He has no chance to read and discuss those notices, those different tickets, those guides to the countryside, those theatre programmes, that other children read, where written words are part of pleasure and excitement and family warmth. Indeed, one of the very first things a child learns to read is not so far away as that – the name of his own street; this is an important part of his own identity and security; emotionally, practically, and satisfyingly, it makes him part of the adult world. Long before the child goes to school, a 'book-mother' will show the child such a name-board, and the two of them may trace the letters with their fingers. But in a London block of Council flats, I have seen two huge official notice-boards bearing the name of the block – one spelling it one way, one spelling it completely differently. Can official contempt on the one side, and confusion on the other, go further?

This child never goes to a bookshop because there are no book-shops in his district, and his parents have neither the time, nor the know-how, nor the money, nor the background, to want to take him to one by bus. He has a Woolworths in his district, perhaps even a Smiths; and very occasionally – maybe once – his mother will buy him a book there.

I once watched a child and his mother in a local branch of Smiths. They were on their way to the market or the shops to do the Saturday morning shopping with Friday's pay, and the mother had called in for her weekly magazine. As they passed a stand of children's books, the child stopped, riveted.

'Mum.'

'What?'

'Mum.' (wriggling) 'I want a book.'

'You can't have one. Come on. I'm in a hurry.'

'Mum.' (pleading) 'I want a book.'

The mother hesitated, mentally reckoning up both money, and time.

'Well, all right. Hurry up then!'

'Hurry up.' The child was confused. (The first child's parents never said this in that Kensington bookshop.) He still tried to hold on to his idea and reached out a hand to a book – a sample.

Mum and passing assistant simultaneously: 'Don't touch!' ('Hurry up' and 'Don't touch.' That first child trotted round the Kensington bookshop and touched about thirty books, looked through twenty, lingered over ten. He spent two hours in that shop. Those two commands made it impossible for this child to find 'his book'.) He put his hands behind his back where they would not get him into trouble, and wriggled a bit, bewildered; how could he deal with this knotted situation? His mother, maddened by this 'unresponsive' child, and aware of the passing of time, snatched a book from the shelf and shoved it at him.

'Here!'

The child, hands behind back, backed away: 'No.' (He knew instinctively this is not how you choose a book.) His mother was now maddened beyond endurance. She had genuinely tried to do her best. He wanted a book, and she had said he could have a book, even though she had not come out intending to buy one – and now he said no. At this point she walloped him, and lugged

him out crying, without a book. She could just as well have in-
sisted he take the book she thrust on him, in which case he would
have gone out of the shop crying, *with* a book . . . a book that was
not *his* book, and that therefore he would never look at – and that
in any case would be ripped to pieces by the smaller children in
the family, because he would have no place that was entirely
his own and nor would the other children, and there would
be no respect or love for books in the family's past experiences;
if it were 'his' book he would have had the heart to fight for it,
to find some way of keeping it safe from the littler ones, but it
isn't.

So his mother will say 'There you are! I knew it was a waste of
money', and buy him lollies or toy tanks in future.

In my own borough of London – Lambeth – we have probably
had for years the best children's librarian in the country, who
organises book corners and story-telling in the parks, in day
nurseries, in Council estates, in swimming baths. . . . A child who
lives within this tiny splinter of streets stands a slightly better
chance of sometimes hearing stories or holding a book; but never
in the permanent, self-assured, physical, participating way every
'book-child' in the country does, who *owns* books, and never with
any place of his own where he can keep a book completely safe,
and therefore dare to love it.

Very few letters come into this child's home. Friends and relatives do not need to be written to since they live nearby – or did
until the authorities uprooted and separated them. (What does
this unchosen uprooting do to people? Or what happens to people
who in order to have amenities that 'the book-child's' family
would take for granted have to give up friendship, affection,
emotional security, and any belief in their own validity?)

Those letters that do come are often authoritative and threatening. They are left unopened as long as possible, eventually opened
with tension, and read with an explosion of anger. It is rarely a
pleasure to get letters in this home.

Letters are rarely written. And the child is rarely encouraged to
add his bit to a letter that goes out (a kiss on the bottom of a
national insurance claim?), and rarely does he receive personally
a part of a letter that comes in. By the time he is five he knows
nothing about reading or writing, or the pleasure of it. The only
emotion words on paper have communicated in his home has been

tension. He doesn't even recognise his own personal name written down, and sees no point in it, gets no pleasure from it, when it is. By five his own identity is already dimmed – and if he still has the initiative to insist on it, it will be with defiance.

Do teachers cuddle?

So then, age five or so, he starts primary school.

If he has until now been going to a day nursery or an unloving minder, with all the deprivation this brings with it, he is from this date going to be even more deprived. Who is now going to look after him when the school day is over, or when school is on holiday? The 'book-child' will be met at school with a warm hug, will go home to tea, and to people who are interested in his doings; this child, at five will be roaming the streets. (He may be very lucky and have a minder who is loving and personal enough to take charge of him again at such times; but no day nursery can step out of line like that. And grandmothers are either far away, because the family has been uprooted, or are working themselves. Many of these five-year-olds literally have to look after themselves.) No-one will talk to him at school, no-one will give him recognition when school is over. And if no-one gives him recognition and draws him into the circle, how can anyone expect him to learn to read or write, since reading and writing is stamping a personal identity on paper?

In his loneliness and isolation, surrounded by bewildering fears, he comes into the playground. There the situation becomes a hundred times worse.

Susan Issacs and Dorothy Gardner observed years ago that children of five to seven rarely of their own accord make groups larger than five. In the school playground this child, who has perhaps been quite isolated for five years by his housing situation, may be thrown among several hundred. In his reception class there will be forty – sometimes fifty – children, many of them bewildered and frightened, because the law requires them to attend school at this age and leave their mothers outside, regardless of how they feel about it, or whether they are ready for this new situation, or of how far they have already been able to explore outside their home.

A frightened child does not speak – though he may want to. He needs someone to speak undemandingly to him, to gently offer herself. If this child is lucky, and gets the maximum personal reading attention possible, he and the teacher may speak *solely with each other* for a total of five minutes per week.

Perhaps if these minutes are given to him in one packet he might be able to ask one question then, and have it carefully answered, in its original form and with all the corollaries that will follow the answer. Entry to school drastically cuts down the number of questions any child can ask in a day and have answered; but this is a child who probably didn't have anyone around to answer questions in the years before he started school, and will not return home to a question-answerer now that he has started school, either.

The whole school situation must be tensely bewildering to him, for unlike the first child he isn't used to being under the constant supervision of one adult, who demands certain performances, often academic or verbal, from him, or expects him to sit down and listen for long periods on end. The first children have known this situation from the time they were born, in cuddly terms when it was part of their love and security, and it is welded into their life. But these kids have managed on their own for a large part of their five years, and have done many things with the supervision perhaps of a sister two or three years older but not of an adult; some of them might accept it now, maybe even gladly, if it were a one to one relationship that went back to the cuddling undemandingness of a secure babyhood and built up from there – but no teacher at an ordinary state school is offering them this.

We could at least bring all the grandmothers, the grandfathers, aunties and uncles, teenagers, people who have no family of their own, and lonely or bored old age pensioners, into the infant schools where they could sit down with a child on their lap and look at a picture book together, and talk. It would not matter in the slightest if their accent was not the same as the teacher's, and if it were more like the child's than like the teacher's it would be preferable. They would be giving this child what the other child has already had for five years – a warm body to lean against, arms to go round him, words linked with smells and physical sensations, read in mutual lingering pleasure for him alone. And instinctively these people will put the child *in* the book. After all, that is what all we adults take for granted. That books are about *us*. That people whom we've never known, who live in centuries past, or countries far away, magically *know* us, and put us in a book. And that in those books, we find dear friends.

It is very easy for children to grasp the real point of reading if it is not distorted for them, and if they have adults with them who delight in it. In May 1973, in the magazine *Books for Your Children* I read this reminiscing letter from Lorna Peterson, of Horndean, Hampshire:

'I began Infants School Libraries in London – in a school set in the midst of a street market. Wonderful open fires in the class-room, central heating in the wide corridors and the halls. . . . One dark winter's day I walked along the corridor, and seeing the library door ajar I peeped in. Two children were there, a boy and a girl, inseparable friends since the day they arrived at school at five years – they were now seven. They were sitting close to the fireguard; the fire was bright, there was a carpet on the floor, pretty Norwegian chairs and tables, flowers on the tables. The children's chairs were touching; the boy held a book and was reading it to the girl, but she had her head on his shoulder and was following his reading. As I crept away, I was saying joyfully to myself that at least two of my children had already learned not only the joy of a book but the joy of sharing.' With all our new technical sophistication, we can scarcely better that. (Do we supply anything like as much?)

For many years I have talked about this all over the country, and been met with horror in London – '*Unqualified* people in the schools!' But in places like Leicester, and further north, and fur-ther south in Cornish villages I was told 'We already do it.' It seems outside London they have managed for a long time to cook a good humoured snook at the union. Is this because they put the needs of these children higher? Or is it because they do not see the children's families so much as The Enemy? Or is it because they are not so desperate to assert their superiority? Are they more part of their community, instead of forming a world of their own?

We could get the children writing letters to each other. They could post them in a letter-box in the classroom that a parent or a friend could make – just as Harry made the one we used in my own nursery school. And when the letters were written to people further away, the school could supply the stamps – they would be much cheaper than reading-machines and audio-visual aids, and unlike these they would be part of the real world – and the children could go out with their teacher to post them, and wait for the postman to collect. . . . (Yes, of course difficulties would be raised about this. It would be 'dangerous', it would need 'insurance', the school couldn't take the responsibility. . . .)

Well, if the union makes it tricky to get the 'unqualified' people these children need into the schools, and if the common-sense ways of giving this large number of children what they have lacked is too difficult for our institutions, at least the first books they are given might help to bridge that gap – might underline their identity, cherish it, and build from there, which after all is one of the many things that has been happening with 'the book-child' for five years. But what is it they are given? They are given readers about a family that lives in a detached house . . . Labrador dog . . . Siamese cat . . . beautiful white damask tablecloth, tea always poured from a graciously sitting position . . . mother who says 'Good morning, children' and children who say 'Good morning, mother' . . . a family who never never has to clock on. If anything could completely confirm for this child what he has already dimly suspected through his growing five years – that he and his family and friends and his street are worthless and expendable – it is the orthodox school reader. As far as they are concerned, he does not exist.

And when he writes his news, or dictates something for his teacher to write down – if he trusts her enough – perhaps it will be something like this

'When Desman comes to slep with my mum I ave to go in the bath in a bed wot my mum puts there When I fall asleep its OK but I don't like Desman he comes ever such a lot of nites to slep and the tap drips.'

(Amber, in Beryl Gilroy's school; described in chapter 23.) And perhaps even a teacher who is so much of a friend to the child that he can write truthfully for her, may be a little disturbed, may even wish he hadn't written it.

Chapter 17

People often talk as though the damage to the child is done only by unknowing parents or by the deprived environment, all of which the school, they say, tries to make good again. On the contrary, the school frequently (sometimes in their own view benignly) delivers the final crushing blow because the conformist school is the main tool of the culture that has deprived, manipulated, restricted and de-validated him for five years. As for those militants who angrily protest at the term 'culturally deprived', I think they are mistaken too; it seems to me a fairly accurate term since the school system is depriving such children of their culture, undermining them under cover of educating them, subduing them by taking away from them the language in which they express emotion, excitement, identity, and power. Scottish Highlanders, Welshmen ... all those whose children have been forced by new law to go to English schools, where they were forbidden to speak their own language and the language of their family and punished if they did, by people who did not belong to the district but ruled in it, know the situation very well.

*I'll tell you
what you like*

Once, in a Preston bookshop that was popular and open in style, I heard a woman's voice say with sadistic zest, 'You just wait till I tell your Dad!'

Curious to know what could happen in a bookshop that could merit this, I turned round. There stood an elderly woman, a grandmother evidently, and a boy, who at the moment was protesting with some spirit. 'But I like it!' he kept saying. 'You just wait till I tell your Dad!' 'But it's funny! It makes me laugh!' 'Oh you just wait – you just wait till I tell him!'

At this point, the boy's mother came in too; she had evidently been busy elsewhere. Immediately the elderly woman said 'He says he wants this book! It says inside it's for four-year-olds!' and the boy's mother instantly turned to him and said, 'You just wait till I tell your Dad!'

The boy kept saying 'But it's funny' (I craned my head, it was a *Paddington Bear* book), but with joint relish, delivering alternate blows, they flattened him out. ('You won't half get it when I tell your Dad!' from one. 'Oh you just wait!' from the other.)

Finally, 'You'll have *this* one! This one's for your age!' and they both triumphantly showed each other the inside of the jacket, nodding their heads in sadistic agreement. (I looked too, expecting I don't know what mighty mountain. It was an Enid Blyton.)

Now these adults had clearly never possessed books themselves. But from somewhere they had got the idea that books were for getting on in the world, for climbing up the ladder, and most definitely not for pleasure. Where else would they have got this from but the school system – with its equivalent of 'Come the

Revolution, you'll have strawberries and cream!' 'But I don't like strawberries and cream!' 'Come the Revolution you'll have strawberries and cream and like it!' Afterwards I thought I should have bought *Paddington Bear* very quickly and shoved it in the kid's pocket before they lugged him out completely, still hopelessly protesting.

I remember how Morag Hunter, whom I met at a conference in Scotland and who at that time had been a remedial teacher in Dumbartonshire, said she kept for her class any miniature, or leather, or funnily-shaped, or locked, or padded books, because the children were interested in books *sensually*; they smelled them, licked them, stroked them. She described how they learned to read in a 'house' they made, lying under the chairs and under the tables, falling asleep on the cushions on the floor, still reading, with sometimes their arms, legs, bodies intertwined with one anothers' – kids who would fight and snarl at physical touch in the playground.

Well, I was once in a magnificent children's bookshop when two primary school teachers came in with seven or eight children whom they'd brought to choose for themselves their end-of-school prizes; and they each had £1.50 to spend. I thought it was wonderful.

The children had obviously never been in a bookshop before; so I eagerly strained my ears to catch every detail of their magic day. I watched them. It *wasn't* wonderful – it was terrible. The children wanted to rush about the shop and explore everything, but the teachers wouldn't allow them to. They wanted to play with the pop-up books – they went straight for the pop-up books – books that were obviously fun; but the teachers wouldn't allow them to. They wanted to look at picture books, the picture books they'd never had when they were kids, but the teachers wouldn't allow them to. They weren't even allowed to buy paperbacks – 'Paperbacks are not books', they were told.

One of the teachers was young, middle-class, trendy, used to bookshops. The other was more working-class, openly more authoritarian, and not used to bookshops.

The first, who was noticeably in command, had a mental list of each child and the book that the child had to choose in order to prove what a good and progressive teacher she was. She picked up a book, opened it, and said, in a voice that rang through the shop and was meant to, 'Here are the testicles, and there's the penis. And this is the vagina, that passage there.' The child, a West Indian girl, was not enthusiastic. The teacher, unaffected, listed other details, '. . . And there's the uterus. *This is what you're interested in.*' No response. The teacher said kindly, explaining, 'This is what you *like*. The human body. That's your subject. I honestly think' (there was something almost touching about this) 'this is a very good book about it.' Pause, while the teacher looked quickly through the book once more to her own satisfaction. Then, 'Will you have this?' The girl listlessly agreed, whereupon the teacher said approvingly 'Good girl! You've chosen a very good book!'

After she had chosen her very good book, I saw this child sitting on a chair in a shut-off reading bay. Away from her teacher, in a little bookshop on her own, she had taken from the shelves a Ladybird book for children just beginning to read, and she was reading it out loud to herself, spelling out each letter as she read.

The trendy teacher didn't see this. She had just taken a displayed book off the shelf, and as a result several other books had fallen over on their sides, and this so terrified the other child who was with her, that the teacher had to say several times that it was all right for this to happen, that books *did* fall over like this, and that you just put them straight again. But this child who needed so much reassurance, who so needed to discover through her own organic experience that handling books brought pleasure not disaster, wasn't left alone with them to browse, and to become familiar and at ease with them. Instead the teacher handed her two books, telling her those were the kind of books she liked – animal books. No suggestion of exploration.

But all the time the other children who had not yet been personally grabbed by the teacher and were not yet intimidated, were running round the shop excitedly, showing each other paperbacks and pop-ups and young children's picture-books. They were full of happiness and amazement and laughter, and were making it quite clear that, in this very first chance they had, they intended to make up for the lost years. And with £1.50 each they could have each found half a dozen paperbacks of their own delighted choosing, a little library of their own for the first time in their life, which they could lend out to each other, so coming voluntarily, in pleasure and kinship, to thirty or forty books – a

wonderfully exciting experience; and this was what they obviously
and naturally wanted to do, and intended to do.

But the second teacher was horrified. She came *running* to the
first. 'He's chosen a pop-up book! He's popping it up and down!
What if he messes it up, and we have to pay for it!' Whereupon
the first said with calm authority 'Oh Robert, don't be silly. You
can't have a book like that!' And when another child pleaded to be
allowed to have a paperback that enchanted him, she said 'No!
You have to find a big, hard-cover book. It must be a book that
lasts *a long time*. If there's anything over after that, you might be
able to have one of those.'

By now all joy was disappearing. The children, whose exuberant
energy till now had been hurtling straight towards the books,
were scuttling and scuffing round in disconsolate self-conscious
hunched-up circles. 'Now look. You've got to decide what *kind* of
books you want. Information or story. Then we'll find the right
shelf, and we'll choose it.' After much prodding of this academically compartmentalised kind, one of the boys who so much wanted pop-ups agreed with great reluctance to say he wanted an
information book, and from there was prodded into agreeing to
say he 'wanted' the particular information book that the teacher
had chosen. 'You really *like* this one, do you?' she said approvingly, and gazing at the pages in a bemused, again rather touching
way, wrapt in some fantasy of her own, she murmured 'You
think you'll use it . . . ?'

Throughout all this, the other teacher, whose spontaneous
reaction was to be much rougher with the kids, was taking her lead
from the first, who 'knew about' children's books, but translating
it into her own language. 'Come *on*! Look for some *hard* books!
(She meant hardbacks, but she kept calling them *'hard'* books').'
No – these are paperbacks! They're for *little* children! Come away!'

They kept going back to them, and she kept literally chasing
them away. She chased them off the paperback stands, and they
went to the pop-ups. She chased them off the pop-ups and they
went to the picture-books. She chased them off the picture-books
and they were back at the paperbacks again. 'You're not supposed
to be reading them! You're supposed to be choosing a book!'

By now the first teacher had managed to persuade each of her
four children to agree to choose the book she herself had chosen,
without losing her temper (indeed, the emotional temperature of

all five of them had come down many degrees) and had left quickly; she evidently hadn't enjoyed the expedition enough to want to stay with her colleague. So her colleague now could openly express herself. 'Either you find a book, or you go back to school! You're just enjoying yourselves! Those are not books! Those are paperbacks! Either you find a book at once, or we go back to school, and you tell Sir why!'

Grumbling and sulking, and each of them minus the £1.50 that had so kindly been allotted to them, they left with their neat packages of books they did not want (but which they had been told were their own choice – and furthermore a 'good' choice).

Of course, as far as these teachers were concerned, the books were not for the child's own growth and joy, but for prestige, to show the adults were successful teachers, that the school was a successful school, and probably also that the parents were successful parents. This is what our schooling has done for us. We all want to get good marks. It was very sad.

But the manipulation of children and the deprivation of their real identity goes much deeper than this.

More state nursery schools, which I have pressed for over many years, will not right this situation unless they *accept* the child and the child's culture and conversation, and show the child that the being *he really is* is important in the world. If they do not, they will merely bring his officially organised annihilation one or two years nearer.

Taking it all in all, is it any wonder that such a child, denied his natural rhythm of growth, and his naturally-learned rhythm of speech, his experience rejected as invalid, his knowledge considered at best disconcerting and unwelcome, the people important to him, with whom he has naturally identified, treated with contempt – is it any wonder that he never learns to read? Or if he does learn, from cold, impersonal, unphysical, unsensuous technique, that is carried out in a special place laid down by law outside his home – learning like a circus dog learns to jump through a hoop to avoid punishment or to please the trainer – is it any wonder that he never looks at a book again once he's left school? If we were honest, would the figures of illiterate, or semi-literate school-leavers, mainly from working-class districts, really be so startling? Frankly, it is often amazing to me that they stay sane.

Gnomes are all right

I had been writing for children – and for adults about children – since the early 1950s, when my books were first published by the Oxford University Press, and I twice was startled, once when 'the gentlemen at Oxford', as my editor John Bell put it, said they would publish my book if I agreed to alter 'bottom' (which occurred three times, I think) to 'behind', and again when my books came out and I found they cost sixteen shillings each, which then was a great deal. I realised I was writing for the elite.

(Fifteen years later I was sitting in a Lancashire folk club, in a large room filled with mothers and fathers and kids, the adults drinking beer and gin-and-tonics, the children orange-squash or coca-cola, and all of them listening with glee to singers whose most frequent two words were 'bum' and 'bugger' and thinking to myself what affectionate familiar and visually recognisable words those were for working-class kids to learn to read from. By then I was no longer writing for the elite.)

Later, in the 1950s, I received another shock. The BBC had just started the 'Listen with Mother' programme and at the beginning I wrote a lot of their material, among it a series of stories about the everyday adventures of a four-year-old called Pete. The first story was broadcast – and was followed by a small avalanche of furious letters, accusing me of undermining society, and demanding to know if they paid their licence fee in order to have their children corrupted. One of them went so far as to list all the wicked things Pete did, such as running instead of walking, going downstairs backwards, arguing, talking to grown-ups who were busy. . . . Their vehemence astounded me. The BBC decided not to do the succeeding stories. (It has been ironic for many years to see this book – for the stories were later published in book form by Methuen – constantly referred to on the dustjacket as 'the best thing that came out of "Listen with Mother",' a quotation from Junior Bookshelf. It certainly did come out of 'Listen with Mother' – fast.)

I was very shocked by these letters, and also by the BBC's reaction to them, for Pete was an ordinary child, and the response he made to his world had been carefully observed and accurately set down; in fact, he was my son. The book has gone into many editions over the years and become very well known and I would say loved; but there are still parents, teachers and librarians who are horrified at it. The interesting thing is that they are in no doubt about its reality. It is reality that frightens them. One of them wrote to me very angrily 'Above all the trouble with it is that every child will *know* Pete is a *real* boy. It wouldn't matter if he was a gnome!'

For many years I turned over in my mind matters like this, and the thoughts I have set down on the preceding pages, together with memories of my own childhood. When late in 1966 Macmillans asked if I would edit a series of supplementary readers for primary schools, and I at first declined, I began to consider if this was the opportunity to do something about a situation I was finding very disturbing, though nobody else seemed very disturbed by it. I went back to Macmillans, and said I would reconsider, if they would consider two things – first, that I had a book coming out that was going to infuriate many important people in education (this was *Risinghill*) and Macmillans might therefore find it embarrassing to have me as an educational editor, and second that if I did edit the series I would only do so on the lines of a briefing I'd prepare which would propose something revolutionary in infant school readers. This was the briefing (I intended to send it to possible authors):

The majority of the children who now read, cannot read about themselves. For with very few exceptions, the children who exist in books are middle-class children. This situation is beginning to change, and a very few books are now being written about working-class streets; of these very few, some

are patronising and 'slumming', others can only be read by
children with educated backgrounds.

School readers are in much the same position. The
children in school readers may not have nannies or house-
keepers or ponies; but they have gardens and lawn-mowers.
What proportion of the readers of these primary school books
actually *do* have gardens and lawn-mowers? . . . or sit down
to a leisurely breakfast with both Mum and Dad? What is it
like when 'children' in some mysterious way apparently does
not include you?

Our whole society is in any case depersonalising these
children. They have never had the space, the pleasant
surroundings, the privacy, the calm, the cherishing, the
respect, the books and pictures and music, the talk and the
discussions and the reading aloud, that have helped other
children's confident identity to grow. And even in the books
they get in school, which are often the only books they
handle, they see no recognition, no reflection of themselves,
nothing that tells them they belong in this world; they grow
up feeling they have no right to exist.

We cannot evade this difficulty – which arises mainly
because our writers are middle-class people with cultured
backgrounds – by making the first books fantasy tales.
Fantasy is fine, important, and enriching – provided it is
rooted on a firm grasp of reality, a firm belief in your own
identity, and a firm confidence that you are worthwhile. We
must give this first, otherwise the fantasy we also want to
give the child will be an escape from the child's own
nothingness, instead of an enrichment of the child's identity.

We must write about our children in primary readers as
they really are. How many writers can do this? And can do
it with accuracy, strength, grace, rhythm – in fact, in good
writing? And have, furthermore, an affectionate and respectful
understanding of the small child – the *essential* child, not
merely the child favoured by circumstances?

Would they, I said, take a fortnight to think about these two
points, and then we could meet again. They did; we did; and they
asked me to edit the series. Though I didn't know it then, this
really was going to educate me.

'My Dad!'

Children's writers in England have always been mainly middle-class, and understandably write about middle-class families in middle-class situations holding middle-class conversations. If you suggested perhaps non-middle-class children might like something they could identify with, they pointed to stories about animals or gnomes. (Many teachers used to do the same.)

I still remember listening to a tape recording at Brian May's Theatre Centre many years ago, in company with other children's writers attending a conference to press for more children's plays. On this tape some comprehensive-school teenagers were discussing theatre. None of these London teenagers had ever been to a theatre in their life. Their ideas of it were groping and nervous. They were sure it was only for rich people. Their phrases were Cockney phrases, and the sentences they expressed these ideas in were not in middle-class structures, and by middle-class grammatical assumptions were often left trailing and unfinished. What they were saying was very important.

The writers, whose children clearly went to prep schools and public schools and were quite familiar with the theatre, found it all most amusing and quaint, and giggled to each other. The comprehensive school kids didn't depress me, but the writers did. I walked out in the middle of the conference, back past the three Council dustbins whose rubbish overflowed all over the pavement where they mingled with the water from the stinking Council lavatories they stood outside, wondering which was more annihilating to these kids and more provocative of destructiveness – the Council or the writers.

So I was not surprised I found it difficult at first to get writers for this new series. (I was to find it was equally difficult to get artists. So many had been trained to draw only Heal's pottery and Habitat chairs and Sunday supplement kitchens, that a milk bottle on the table and a spoon stuck in a packet of sugar made them very nervous.) And I eventually decided to write the first stories myself. I spent a lot of time at Brixton market in South London, visited several schools in the East End of London where, when I asked where they went on Sundays, the child said that her Mum said you don't go nowhere when you've got ten children, and where I looked through a child's schoolbook where she had written – and got warm praise for – a story that began 'There was a little girl, and she lived in a cottage in a wood,' and I said to her 'What's a cottage?' 'I don't know.' 'What's a wood, then?' 'I don't know.' 'Have you never been in a wood, then?' 'No.' And where what's called a garden turns out to be a backyard (what book-children casually call a garden is here called very specifically 'a garden with things growing') and where 'the park' is the tiny *concrete* playground. A child told me with great pride that they had a window-box 'and we brought back two daffodils and we planted them and they grew again two years later'. *Two* daffodils! Only two years!

So I wrote a group of stories about a family I called the Carter family. (My own notes for these stories ran: 'Mum is an office-cleaner, part-time. Dad works in a hospital as boiler-man, some-times on day-shift, sometimes on night-shift. He works twelve-hour shifts, but sits down a lot of the time. One boiler is out, for maintenance, now and then, while the other boiler is on. He maintains, polishes, cleans, watches gauges for temperature – a responsible job (about £15 a week?). Has tool-box with hammers, spanners, screw-drivers, polish cloths. They live in a house that's been condemned for years. Eventually they will be rehoused, in a house the Council has taken over and done up for a big family. Around them, blocks of flats are going up – too small for them.' Since the stories were to be about the children, these notes were mainly to keep my own mind clear. But looking back at them now, what a far cry they were from the orthodox children's reader. I also drew a map of their imaginary district, with all the landmarks – streets, primary school, fire-station, adventure playground, Woolworths, and so on – marked in. Since the stories – though I don't think anyone has ever noticed it – intertwine, each telling the adventure of one of the children on that same afternoon, it was important that all the action was geographically possible.)

I typed out five of them, and took them to one of the East End schools to try out. As I read the first story to a child at the back of the class, the young teacher, passing by, heard it and was very intrigued. This was not the sort of story that Infant Schools generally had. She asked me to stay all day in the school instead of the morning as I'd planned, and tell the whole class the stories after dinner.

It was an extraordinary experience. I described it in *Look at Kids*, and what follows is almost the same words. From the first sentence the children began to laugh, and they never stopped laughing. At first I thought I'd wait till they stopped before I went on to the next sentence; but this was impossible, since they never stopped. I had to read on through the laughter. This was a kind of laughter I had never heard from children before. These kids were all up on their feet, jumping up and down, hugging themselves, hugging each other, tears – tears of laughter – streaming down their faces, and they were shouting out 'It's my Dad! It's my Dad!' or 'My Mum says that, my Mum!' They were laughing helplessly, not just with their mouths or their faces but with their entire bodies as if they were babies, and these bodies, jumping and hugging in front of me, visibly grew limper and softer, more and more floppy and relaxed, all tension shaking out of them with the jumping and the hugging and the laughter. I was actually very shaken myself – I'd never seen anything like this outside the family circle before, and this was happening on a large scale. All the time it was going on (and every time I finished a story they demanded another, so I had to read every story I'd brought) all the time it was going on I was thinking, 'What *is* this? What's happening?' I was still thinking this all the way home, at the end of the day, completely bemused.

Waiting for me was a letter from a head in Kettering to whom I had sent a typescript of another story I had written – *Fish and Chips for Supper* – and his report of the scene in his classroom where he had read this out was identical with the East End one. He said one boy, whose father was 'just the amiable layabout Dad of your story', was trying very hard to explain to the boy next to him, whose father was a stern conscientious worker-type, why the story was so funny and so important to him, but was laughing so much he could only jump up and down, tears streaming down his cheeks and gasp out 'It's my Dad! It's my Dad!'

Standing with his letter in my hand and considering all this, my mind went back to the evening I had seen the play *Billy Liar* in a West End theatre. 'Seen' is accurate since I could scarcely hear a word. I was extremely annoyed at the time. The laughter was continuous, drowning all dialogue, and completely physical; I came out of that theatre not only angry and frustrated since I am very fond of the play, but bruised all over from the helpless back-slapping and knee-thumping and yankings I'd been subjected to from delirious hefty strangers who shouted at me, their eyes helplessly streaming. (It was at this time that Albert Finney, playing Billy, who understood the phenomenon as little as I did then, walked to the footlights and said furiously 'If you lot don't shut up, I'm going home!' The press discussed this quite a bit at the time – such an event was unprecedented.)

All the time in the theatre I was looking with bewilderment at this coach-party audience and wondering '*Why* are they laughing like this? Why is it so funny to them that Billy's father says "bloody" in front of every other word when they do it themselves all the time? It isn't as if it's *strange* to them!'

Now I put the three experiences together, and it suddenly clicked. What I had heard was the astonishingly helplessly physical laughter of release from tension, the laughter of acceptance, of recognition. For the first time with a shock of delight those children, and those adults, had seen themselves portrayed in preserves that hitherto were middle-class and alien. They didn't have to pretend to be someone else any more. They were released.

Not only did this release and acceptance in the classrooms – this startled joyful recognition of phrases and situations – turn books into friends, and make the whole business of learning to read *affectionate*. But in the relation it produces, – because you're *there*, you're *known*, you're *accepted* – is the beginning of growth, spreading out. I've never forgotten that day.

Filthy
fish and chips

At the beginning of 1967 – still before the Plowden Report – when I had collected some stories by other writers too, we sent out 'dummies' (no pictures, no covers) to twenty schools all over the country, asking for reports from both the staff and the children.

They were stories made from perfectly ordinary working-class ingredients. But the first reports that came back were scandalised, and vehement. The heads and teachers said that such subjects should not be mentioned. They also said that such subjects did not exist. They said children did not play on bomb-sites or dumps; there were no bomb-sites or dumps; they had all been built over long ago. All children played in parks or pleasant play areas. No children played in old cars. All homes had hot and cold water and proper bathrooms. And nobody used tin baths.

These remarks were made by heads and teachers, who actually taught in areas where the children always played in the local dump and in the old cars, and had homes without hot water, and used tin baths; they made them hostilely. They were also made by progressive university educationists who quite amiably asked 'But does any child play on a bomb-site or a rubbish dump now? Have children of today ever seen tin baths?'

Two stories in particular – *Fish and Chips for Supper* and *Going to Bed*, both of them light-hearted and very rhythmic, and not at all bleak – sent them into a frenzy. They said they were 'slum situations' and 'ridiculous' and 'silly'. (They used this last adjective frequently, English fashion, to express moral outrage.) Both of these stories involved someone in bed. One was focused on Dad

in bed, refusing to get up and go to work and messing things up
for everyone (and ended with the irate mother pulling the sheets
off him). The other had two small children, boy and girl, who
slept in the same bed. I had a strong impression at the time that
a bed could only figure in a school reader if it was uninhabited by
human beings (a teddy or a rabbit or a gnome might have been all
right).

As for the first story I became aware for the first time that 'fish
and chips' – merely the phrase – was a symbol almost equivalent
to 'gin'. Also, they instantly talked angrily about fish and chip
shops, apparently leaping to the conclusion that people who spoke
and behaved as these could only be eating fish and chips that had
been cooked in a fish and chip shop (equivalent to a Victorian gin
palace) which was immoral, whereas characters who spoke and
behaved differently would have cooked their own fish and chips at
home (although I had never said these didn't), or had them in a
restaurant, with Hollandaise sauce, which was moral. I was
startled to find this was picked on as an issue, let alone such a
passionate one. Did fish and chips (which emotionally they were
sure came from a fish-and-chip shop) represent feckless lazy
parents as against hard-working Puritanical teachers? Or did it
remind them of the number of children who were at that time
slipping out of schools at dinner-time in order to spend their
school dinner-money at the chippy down the road, like relaxed
adults rather than supervised kids? And how did it happen that
people who probably gave infant-school science lessons on food
values were thrown into such rage at the thought that their children might possibly get something really nutritious and body
building. (In fact, only a minority would reach that peak; most
would just have chips.) I was bemused.

The second story, which was about a small boy, age about
three, who'd got 'filthy dirty' playing in the dump, having a bath
in the tin bath in front of the fire, then joining his sister in bed
when he's 'clean as a daisy', also caused a great deal of anger. The
phrase 'filthy dirty' was vehemently attacked for some reason
which I've never fathomed – perhaps because by teachers' logic,
which I gradually learned, to say a child is 'filthy dirty' means you
are *telling him to be* filthy dirty; though I had a feeling it was
something to do with the grammar of the idiom; and tin baths,
they said, didn't exist. Nothing was actually written down by them

about this little boy and girl sharing a bed, but the number of 'silly's' hurled about like grenades seemed to say it was too shocking to bring into the open.

Many of them castigated me for bringing 'swearing' into infant schools. I was perplexed. I ferreted into this, and discovered they meant one child saying to another child 'shut up'.

'Cheeky children do not need to be encouraged!' they said. This meant they didn't like to see children's normal conversation with one another reproduced in print. As in adult books, the characters in *Nippers* talk in the way they would really talk. Children talk like children, East-End fathers talk like East-End fathers, teachers talk like teachers. This made the teachers say the stories were illiterate, and ugly, 'like comics'.

They were very angry with another story – Jill Bavin's *Saturday Morning*. They were already angry because the boy in it played in the local dump, called the Deb-ree (the local name in the district where Jill Bavin taught), where he usually found treasure – a magnet, or an old car, or an ants' nest; dumps they said, repeatedly, did not exist, whatever the children called them. But what made them even more angry was that he liked to feel the ache in the back of his legs when he ran up the ten flights of stairs to his flat, and the ache in the front of them when he ran down. They felt he had no right to this self-awareness and interest which they called 'disgusting' and 'silly'.

Now a baby, a child, is in constant touch with himself. A baby, boy or girl, used to being without nappies, will happily discover genitals, as earlier he discovered fingers, and pull them about with pleasure and delight. His mouth eagerly, his nose gravely, is constantly in touch with everything, savouring it. Look at Christy, this child who happens to be standing near me as I write. At four-and-a-half, he drains his orangeade, and swiftly wipes his mouth with the whole of the back of his arm from shoulder to finger-tip. An adult would daintily touch her lips with a handkerchief, probably using only one deprecating finger, and that draped. A small child is not afraid of his body, but delights in it and is in touch with it. We are afraid. A teacher is afraid of the ache in the leg, or afraid of pleasure in the body, and has forgotten that both the ache and the pleasure are the same thing – awareness.

I remember once I was among a crowd of sixteen-year-old boys, one of whom had started to comb his hair, which led to mass barracking and horsing around and mock-fighting and mock-strangling, in which some of the boy's own saliva dripped on to his jacket. Shouting now louder than ever, he touched it with his comb – and suddenly he was making silvery-stranded patterns over his body in rapt absorption, silently lost in beauty, like a two-year-old. Of course a teacher then stepped in, yelled 'What the hell d'you think you're doing!' and gave him a blow on the face that knocked him across the room.

But to return to these stories: these teachers were unanimous that the stories were 'in very bad taste' (unlike *Janet and John. Janet and John's* introductory book specifically claims that 'the subject matter fits the child's experience and psychological development and is always in good taste'); equally strongly they said the children agreed with them completely and were 'shocked' to hear the teachers read such stories, and to hear such things (which anyway didn't exist) mentioned.

When the rest of the reports from schools came in some time later – three times as many as the first batch; the angry ones, of course, rushed to the attack – we were relieved to see that they said the opposite: that at last someone was writing stories about what was really happening, about situations the children recognised instantly, and furthermore was writing in a style that was 'vivid', 'vigorously imaginative' and 'poetic'; and, equally emphatically, that the children *loved* them.

Out of curiosity I checked the areas, wondering if it was in working-class or middle-class ones that heads were hostile – and found that hostile heads covered similar districts to enthusiastic heads, sometimes even adjacent and slightly overlapping districts. It was a matter of the personality of the head, rather than social area.

What appalled and angered me was, first, that the first heads were actually invalidating the children's real experience. And what was even worse, far, far worse, they were training the children (who they said 'were shocked') to invalidate it too. This was like the teacher who told the children which books they 'wanted'. You can't train children to deny the truth about themselves, and then expect them to enjoy books. For that is the subject of books.

The appalling accusative

Then one after another came official reports (notably the Milner–Holland housing report) and articles in the national press and television documentaries (one of them showing the tin baths hanging on the yard walls and the children being bathed in front of the fire in a Nottingham area where, it was stated, nine out of ten houses had no bathroom and eight out of ten no indoor lavatory), and finally the Plowden Report. Experts revealed that the dump round the corner did exist. We wondered if, amazingly, we would become respectable.

In January 1969 we published fourteen titles. What I was aiming at was that every child throughout the country, whatever his background, whether urban, rural, or suburban, and whatever his family culture, would be able to find at least one story that recognised and reflected his own family, his family relationships, his district, his language, which he could read over and over again, and which would give him the belief in himself to read on.

I knew of course that 'at least one' was not nearly enough. But there were so many situations, so many communities, utterly unrecognised by infant school books, that I couldn't possibly touch on each separately, even once; I could only give a taste here and there. And even this taste could not be written in such local idiom that it was incomprehensible to children from other districts. I could only go after the rhythm and tune of an idiom, with an occasional specific local word, and the physical and economic situation and emotional attitude of the area. *Nippers* were to be a national publication. I came quite quickly – reluctantly realising the limitations as well as the important path-finding possibilities of *Nippers* – to decide that as well as *Nippers* completely local books needed to be got out by local community groups of all kinds.

The anger that had been roused by the 'dummies' showed me joltingly that many heads would find real *white* children difficult enough to accept. I decided regretfully to leave real *non-whites* (who, whatever Powellites might say, were fewer, and would in any case profit from the first victory), for the second wave. So there were no non-white children in the very first stories – they came later; to me the gap stood out a mile, and I could only hope it wouldn't be so disturbingly obvious to anyone else. We started to fill this gap with the second batch, and later ones, though this had proved very difficult; I had to try one approach after another, and the break was eventually made through John la Rose's Caribbean New Beacon Bookshop – we at least had West Indian writers with their own emotional attitudes and experiences flowing into their sentences, as well as West Indian characters.

We picked out two of the titles and sent one or other as a free sample to schools all over the country. One was Mary Cockett's *Frankie's Country Day*, a very pleasant story (lushly illustrated by Mary Dinsdale) of a city boy seeing the countryside for the first time, told in a way that is readily acceptable to teachers. The other was my *Fish and Chips for Supper*, a light-hearted story in traditional folk-story style, with funny cartoony pictures by Richard Rose. I print it here in order that the reactions can be evaluated.

One day,
as Dad got out of bed,
a drip fell down from the ceiling,
and wet his head.

'Ow,' he said
And he hid under the sheets.

Dad, Dad, go to work.
Then you can bring home your pay.
And we can have fish and chips
for supper.

I can't go to work.
I can't get out of bed.

A drip fell on me,
and wet my head.
Get a bucket.

Bucket, bucket, catch the drip.
Then Dad can go to work.
Then he can bring home his pay.
And we can have fish and chips
for supper.

I can't catch the drip.
I'm full of washing.
Get it out.

Washing, washing,
get out of the bucket.
Then the bucket can catch the drip.
Then the drip won't fall on Dad.
Then Dad can go to work.
And he can bring home his pay.
And we can have fish and chips
for supper.

I can't get out.
I've no line to hang on.
Stretch out the line.

Line, line, stretch over the stairs.
Then the washing can get out
of the bucket.
And the bucket can catch the drip.
And the drip won't fall on Dad.
And Dad can go to work.
And he can bring home his pay.
And we can have fish and chips
for supper.

I can't stretch over the stairs.
The stairs are too dark.
Switch on the light.

Light, light, switch on.
Then the line can stretch
over the stairs.
And the washing can get out
of the bucket.
And the bucket can catch the drip.
And the drip won't fall on Dad.
And Dad can go to work.
And he can bring home his pay.
And we can have fish and chips
for supper.

I can't switch on.
The bill isn't paid.
Pay it.

Mum, Mum, pay the bill.
Then the light can switch on.
And the line can stretch
over the stairs.
And the washing can get out
of the bucket.
And the bucket can catch the drip.
And the drip won't fall on Dad.
And Dad can go to work.
And he can bring home his pay.
And we can have fish and chips
for supper.

But Mum said, 'How can I?
'How can I pay the bill
when your Dad stays in bed?
'Get up.
'Get up and go to work.
'Get up and get your pay.
'Get up at once.'
And she pulled back the sheets.

So Dad got up.

And he went to work.
And he got his pay.
And Mum paid the bill.
And the light switched on.
And the line stretched
over the stairs.
And the washing got out of
the bucket.
And the bucket caught the drip.
And the drip didn't fall
on Dad any more.
And we all had fish and chips
for supper.

The heads were still battling. The first flood of angry letters said vehemently that the story was *immoral*. ('Immoral'? Thus referred back to it, I was surprised to see that both in story-line and in shape it was surely one of the most moral stories ever written.)

They went on:

'I must express my complete dislike of the world portrayed in your latest readers. Most working-class families have now reached what was previously a middle-class environment and standard of living. Even during the depression very few reached the depths of squalor depicted in your books – iron bedsteads were discarded years ago in most homes. Washing in buckets and lines slung across stairs, the hallmark of slums. If Plowden suggests leaving the upper strata of society – at least let us not descend completely to the gutter. Better let our children aim for the stars than rush headlong to degradation.' (The home in the story is in fact – in very, very mild infant-school terms – the London home (Islington 1965) I described in *Risinghill* (Penguin, 1969), pp. 44–8, and was typical of that area.)

'The Plowden Report, which like the Curate's Egg, good in parts, made many false premises. Most children's books today are beyond reproach. . . . They do not postulate a lazy father and a sluttish mother (in my text she was certainly not 'sluttish', and she was portrayed by Richard as neat,

charming, and pretty) but give a child something for which
to strive. God forbid that the situation in this book is the
norm for the "working-classes". Perhaps they provide some
interest in the Gorbals, although I believe children brought
up under such conditions should not be reminded of them . . .'

'This kind of attitude, of children shouting at parents –
listening too much to parents' business – non-payment of
bills – father too lazy to go to work, is not one to be
perpetuated through reading, and is in effect a levelling down
of standards undesirable in any school. Even in this middle-
class area we have to overcome the background of children
ruling the roost at home – we do not want to encourage it.'

'I have perused (your publication) in the spirit of the
Plowden recommendation. . . . The illustrations are, no
doubt, excellent in the strip cartoon context, but the social
content does not, as your intention, reflect the personal
experience of the average child. The moral content, in my
opinion, is degrading. Ask yourself: Did your father stay in
bed, and allow the roof to leak? Do you hang washing on the
stairs and light the house with unshaded lamps? Do not
underestimate the penetration and susceptibility of the young
intelligence. Try again and endeavour to set a standard that
the youngster can emulate to his profit.'

'I have an old fashioned abhorrence of throwing away books,
but on the other hand, have no wish to retain such a book in
school. I work in a district where the sentiments, language
and moral values tend to a degree to be those of *Nippers*,
but that does not seem to me a valid reason to present these
values to the children in school, where we hope they will
learn manners and a correct sense of values. Last week I
spoke to a teenage boy from this background and his
comment – "you can look up to your teacher if not to your
Dad" seems to me to sum up the feelings I have against this
book. We are here to educate "up" not "down".'

'We realise that not all children own ponies, etc., but neither
do they live in houses with holes in the roof, have fathers
who have to be pleaded with by their offspring to go to work

(this is reminiscent of the Victorian melodrama or the Band
of Hope literature forty years ago) hang their washing on the
stairs or live on a perpetual diet of fish and chips. To carry
on this idea to its logical conclusion no doubt some of the
books must contain phrases like "Drink up your meths, Dad"
or "Sis, Sis, smoke your 'pot'." Even if the series is intended
for deprived children with an extremely poor home
environment it would be better to try to raise their sights a
little so that they realise that there *are* better ways of living
and that life does not consist entirely of fish and chips and
the junk yard. Surely it must be enough for them to *have* to
drag father out of bed before they go to school, without
having to read about it when they get there. . . .'

'It is many years since I taught in the slums of Birmingham
and London and I think as I did then that everything should
be done to give these youngsters an opportunity of rising
above their environment. The morals of the book are
completely wrong – lazy father – unpaid electricity bills and
making fish and chips a treat. . . . At my next head-teachers'
meeting I shall raise the issue of this series and I can assure
you that not one will find its way into this school. . . .'

'The head of the family should not be made the object of
criticism. Even in families where the father might be lazy,
it does not help to have the point driven home. . . .'

'It conveys a wrong sense of values and poor standards of
behaviour to the child. I have rarely seen a more unsuitable
book for any child in any social class whatever.'

'It epitomises the very faults which we try to combat in
school, the demands instead of the asking, the statement of
facts. Our children I admit do live in this way, they do not
say please and thank you, they demand and accept as their
right, this I think is what we most object to in the language
of the book. . . .'

One head sent the book back, with a ring round every 'And'
at the start of a sentence. I admired her application. I turned to
the end of the book, expecting to see 'See me', but she spared me
that; so I pointed out to her that a book I suspected she used

respectfully with her school began practically *every* sentence with 'And' – the Book of Genesis.

I showed the letters to Peter Pickering, who later wrote the *Nipper*, *Uncle Norman*, and had himself been a teacher, and asked him why teachers and heads were so angry with *Fish and Chips for Supper*. He read it through and said 'Well, it's obvious. They identify with the father – the authority.' And I showed it to another friend, Malcolm Johnson, a designer, asking him why teachers were also angry with Richard Rose's pictures, and again he said 'It's obvious. Those kids are unkillable, aren't they?' The trouble was, *Nippers* stirred in such teachers awareness of a conflict between reality and what they were trained to teach.

A teacher – a really warm good teacher, I would say – came up to me when I had talked at some conference when *Nippers* were still new – and said she was genuinely delighted with them (and I believe her). She had sat among the children, she said, and they read the stories together and laughed till the tears ran down their faces, just as I had described – and then, she said, *she was filled with panic*. Before she came to this conference, she had been reading with them the first story about the Carter family, where Jimmy who is too little to reach the front door bell is trying to get someone to let him in. He tried various methods.

> He tried standing back
> and trying to run up the door.
> But all that happened was
> that he left dirty marks all over the door.
> And a nail fell out of the number.
> After this, instead of saying 3,
> it said Ɛ.

In the middle of her genuine laughter, a voice in her head had suddenly said 'He *shouldn't* leave dirty marks on the door!' and she was paralysed and terrified. How could she deal with this emotional conflict, she asked me. At the time, beyond offering a few genuinely friendly words, I didn't take her dilemma very seriously; I have thought of it often ever since.

Many teachers, less warm and open-hearted, more totally trained, didn't even allow this conflict to surface. They blandly disengaged themselves. At the same conference another teacher came up to me, also assured me that she agreed with everything I said and thought *Nippers* were an excellent series – 'for *some* children'. But 'there are no fish and chip shops in my district, and neither I nor my children have ever seen one.'

'Where do you live, then?' I said to her, thinking she must come from some remote little island.

'Clapham,' (Clapham is in South London) she answered. Very shaken, I stammered, 'But I am sure there are fish and chip shops there.'

'No,' she said, calmly and sweetly, 'there are none. None at all,' and moved away.

Above all, of course, the fact that the child-readers *recognise* the characters (Back to *Little Pete* again – 'It wouldn't matter if he was a gnome!') and *laugh*, is very frightening to some adults. Laughter, and art, can be deeply threatening to many teachers, who feel very precarious even among pomposity. That a new and more fulfilling safety lay in joining in the laughter was beyond their life training. For training and schooling aim at preserving the status quo, whereas *Nippers*, springing on the contrary from creativity, rocked it.

I should perhaps at this point say that, somewhat to our surprise, we found within ten months of actually publishing that we had sold more than a quarter of a million – remarkable for a reader. The pattern of the try-out was repeating – the immediate vociferous anger from a minority, then the delighted (and less vocal) response from a majority. ('We laughed till we cried, the children and I.' This phrase was to turn up over and over again from heads and teachers. Always *'we'* from these schools, meaning the adults and the children, in affectionate unity. And 'I love this story! That's my Dad! My Mum says that!' kept turning up, from children.)

It was easy to laugh at the letters – almost impossible not to – until you remembered that each letter represented an attitude towards the identity of several hundred captive children and their families. For it was clear that children in quite a few primary schools were still ruled by a head who did not want to know what their life was like – who saw the children as bad – who equated deliberate blindness with morality and virtue – who believed that only exhortations and propaganda should be put before children (and therefore, by authoritarian logic, that whatever was mentioned *was* an exhortation, either a moral one or an immoral one) –

who invalidated the children's experience – trained them, in the guise of self-respect and respect for adults, to despise their parents, their roots, and themselves – who could not face real relationships – felt pitiably insecure in a very shaky social hierarchy and therefore held on to pomposity – who found it impossible to grasp the unity, and therefore the meaning, of a story – and had absolutely no sense of humour. What does this do to children's learning – and to their living?

In 1972 we launched *Little Nippers*, very simple stories, not so much narratives as prose-poems, that aimed to capture concisely, delicately, and very simply some emotional situations involving relationships. (I am analysing after the event. *Nippers* and *Little Nippers* were written intuitively.) The pictures, which even more than in *Nippers* were done with strong editorial direction but in creative partnership with the words, picked up what had been hinted at in, or formed the basis for, the text. Again, the stories were all actuality – children observed, children overheard.

I had been to a school in South-West London, where the kids talked to me all the time about 'The Projectile'.

'Went up Projectile Saturday.' 'Saw a bloke, a tramp, in Projectile. Had to stay till seven at night, waiting for him to go.' 'We build camps in Projectile . . . with wood boxes thrown over from the old people's home.' There are 'bricks, bushes, ladybirds, lizards, tiny frogs in Projectile.' 'We play in old houses. Get wood out of it. Wooden floorboards. We take 'em in Projectile.' 'There's a place in Projectile where they used to make bombs. The kids used to find them. . . .'

'We found two suitcases in Projectile with travelling clocks and clothes in them. . . . We found three fire extinguishers under the ice. . . .' 'We built a raft in Projectile. . . .' 'There was a stolen car in the Projectile. The police came and towed it away. . . .' 'We took all the seats out of this car in the Projectile and made a camp. . . .'

'There are trees . . . logs . . . and fungus there. . . .' 'I saw a squirrel run up a tree . . . and a fox – or a cat. . . .' 'We're going to build a house in the Projectile, and we've cut down the bushes. . . .' 'Three white butterflies came down. . . .' 'There are cabbage white and red admirals there. . . .' 'And finches and tiger moths, orange and black . . . and I saw two kestrels, or sparrow hawks. . . .'

I asked the head what the Projectile was, and he said it was the local dump, the site of an abandoned armaments factory – Projectile and Engineering Company – that had grown and grown with every war. The local families had worked there for generations, grandparents, great-great-grandparents, fathers and mothers. But now it was moving up to the Midlands, dropping its workers, the kids' parents, in the dole queue. Its forty-foot wall that had belched fumes from cooled tempered steel all over the school windows for as long as anyone could remember had recently been demolished, and light had flooded into the school, amazing everyone. But the Projectile – this dump that teachers (not teachers from this school, which was in a dilapidated building, but was wonderfully warm and human, but teachers who cared more for the outsides of things) said didn't exist, was part of memory, and very important; and right now it was the place where without teachers they learned every subject that school was supposed to teach, and were fascinated. There was danger there too, of course, and I don't just mean the bomb-cases. One part had been blocked off because the sewers were being worked on; some adults had been into it to dump rubbish without enough responsibility to block it off again, and a little girl in a snow-white nylon-fur coat – Christine – had trailed along behind and slipped down a manhole. When the head helped fish her out 'her nylon fur weighed a ton.'

The Head – Mr C. J. R. Grubb – told me that the six-year-olds in the school were often left alone in the evenings to look after the younger ones while Mum went out cleaning (there has always been a tradition here of mothers working) or to Bingo. And in the same way the six-year-olds have to take the littler ones to the doctor when they are ill. 'If there's good will', he said, 'between the family and us, I write an explanatory letter for the child to take. But sometimes there isn't, and then the six-year-old tells the doctor what's wrong with the baby, for the doctor to prescribe.'

So I wrote a *Little Nippers*, mostly pictures, about a child going to the doctor's on his own. (I didn't have him taking a younger child, feeling that perhaps teachers could only stand my going halfway to reality.)

'I wish my Mum was here.
'I wish my Dad was here.
'I wish my big sister was here.
'I wish that old man would stop coughing.

Chapter 22

'I wish these comics weren't all torn.

'I wish I wasn't at the doctor's by myself.

'Now it's me. I wish it wasn't. What will he do to me?

'He's listening, listening to my heart.

'And *I'm* listening! Listening to *his* heart!

'And I'm listening, listening to *my* heart, my own heart, with this thing – a stethoscope.

'I can hear it! Kerplunk kerplunk kerplunk. Thumping and tramping like a giant with hob-nail boots.

'We're giants! I like that doctor. He's great!'

A head responded by writing to Macmillans, 'I hope Leila Berg and yourselves enjoy the money you make from pandering to the de-moralisation of our language and society.'

And a letter from another headmaster denounced 'the vulgarisms' in this story 'where we find repeated errors connected with the subjunctive; *I wish my mum was here.* "Was" should be replaced by "were". This is followed by the appalling use of the accusative with the verb "to be" – "*Now it's me!*" '

It is asking a lot, but for the moment, let's confine ourselves to the grammatical question. If the kind of education this man believes in works, surely after a century of it we would all be saying 'It is I' and 'I wish my mum were here' – whereas it isn't even said by all the middle-class kids who have the most solid and longest stretches of education of all, and whom this man imagines to be his loyal cohorts – 'Children who have acquired good pre-school speech habits,' he says, 'do not use the semi-literate forms of expression used in these books, and if, on joining school their speech should deteriorate to the level of the text of these books, parental wrath would soon reach the unfortunate Headteacher.' – let alone the kid who kicks and thumps on the front door because he hasn't got a key and his mum is working. ('Who *is* it?' yells someone, throwing up a window. 'It is I!') Perhaps in the whole English-speaking world this small handful of angry heads are the only people who say 'It is I', dodos in positions of leadership.

But when it really sinks in – that what this particular head of a school of several hundred small children finds appalling is not that a five- or six-year-old has to go to the doctor's surgery alone, but the use of the accusative with the verb to be – then my memory goes back to Henry Reed's poems and 'the point of balance which we have not got', and I find myself shuddering.

Because this is the difference that decides whether kids learn to read or not. Not the difference between various reading techniques, but the differences in attitudes to the children and the children's own community and the children's lives, and what makes sense to those children.

If you exclude from a child everything that makes reading meaningful – his own speech, his parents' speech, his friends' speech, comics, genuine letters, his spontaneous comments on things that have happened, football pools, matches, Gran dying, visits to hospital – all the things he genuinely enjoys and the things he genuinely hates or is frightened of, if you state you are appalled at his colloquialisms, if you call the content of his life 'disgusting rubbish', why should he confide speech to paper – and ever read or write?

There are many teachers who think they invented language. Or else perhaps that God invented it, and handed it down to teachers on Mount Sinai. They seem to be unaware that each separate child invents language for himself, and in conjunction with the people who are closest to him, in his own home, develops it, so that he can communicate his needs and his emotions to these Important People.

A baby learns to walk in his own home, without anyone but himself teaching him. He lies on his back and waves his arms and legs . . . he lies on his front, squirming and scrabbling. One day, striving with all his being like this, he moves – but in a circle. He is not defeated, but makes even greater efforts. One day his legs learn to push . . . one day his arms learn to pull . . . and one day he is hauling himself on his stomach over the floor. He is not satisfied. He works away, till he has discovered how to move on his hands and knees (and what speed he develops!) . . . then on his hands and feet, his bottom stuck up in the air like a dog snuffling after a beetle. Till one day, pulling himself up by the un-'educational' furniture of his own home, or the clothes of his own Important People, he stands – holding on. Soon he can move all round the room by holding on to these objects that are there simply because they are part of his life. Then for one breathless second he stands alone, legs straddled, arms out to keep balance – an evolutionary miracle repeated all over the world millions of times a minute. And soon he is lurching forward, holding his Important Person's hand. All this he has accomplished by the time he is about one year old, practising of his own free will every waking minute of every day, with so much zest and energy that it almost overwhelms an adult, using all the familiar things in his own environment, encouraged by admiration and drawn by people, objects and events that are interesting to *him* – and not a teacher in sight.

Suppose when he came to school at the age of five, having been forced by law to do so, his teachers said to him, 'There is only one correct way to walk, and you are doing it wrong. Every time you walk I shall point this out to you, or pretend not to see that you have walked up to me because I refuse to recognise your way of walking.' Would you be surprised that after a while maybe 25,000 children do not walk very well or with much confidence or pleasure, or perhaps have stopped walking at all . . . and have become rather sullen and hostile? Instruction might even defeat Evolution.

Chapter 23

What is a sprout?

I have always been amazed that anyone who doesn't speak middle-class well-educated English ever learns to read at all.

Listen to these people on this South London bus. Two kids are wrangling over a comic on the seat in front of me. 'Lesshaerlook!' says one to the other. A woman catches sight of a friend across the aisle and is surprised, 'Wens you come up?' she calls. On the platform two teenage boys are arguing. 'Nah-woofawthen?' says one. And a young woman dashes on to the bus as a shower begins – 'EE-ah-ow! A gi' aw we' ah wiww!' ('Ow! I'll get all wet, I will!' said very fast. I don't really know how to set it down. But I want to show how different what they say really is from the sounds they are supposed to read and *recognise as their language*.)

Now in a school reader, no children in any case would either have a comic, or would wrangle; but in no circumstances whatever would they say 'Lesshaerlook!' They wouldn't even say 'Let's have a look!' or even 'Let us have a look!' They'd say 'Please let me see.' (Actually they wouldn't. I'm being too kind. They'd say 'See John, see.')

The woman who said 'Wens you come up?' wouldn't even appear in a reader, but if she appeared in an ordinary children's story that reached an infant school, she would say 'When did you get on?'

The teenagers, non-existent in a reader but possibly appearing in a story, would say 'Why?'

And the young woman who wanted to get out of the rain and expressed this with such infectious zest, exuberance and vitality – what would she say? I'm lost here. Because if you translate the

sentence into approximate middle-class English – for instance
'Oh dear, I shall get wet' – you have something so gutless and
lifeless and idiotic that it would stand out even in an orthodox
infant reader.

I was standing outside a sea-lion enclosure with Martha and
Emily the other day. All around me people were exclaiming 'Don't
he *move*!' or just occasionally, 'Doesn't he *move*!' Middle-class
people would have said 'Doesn't he move *fast*!' They might
specify the adverb differently – 'Doesn't he move *gracefully* . . .
sinuously . . .', enriching their language by thoughtful accuracy;
but surely the intense concentratedness of 'Don't he *move*!' has a
richness too, of a different kind; and only a teacher who was so
bound up with our schooling system as to be forced into stupidity
would feel driven to say it was meaningless, or could as easily
denote slowness as speed; yet many will do exactly this.

As a child in Salford, who read voraciously, I remember how
disconcerted and humiliated I was to realise that 'sword' was
pronounced 'sawd', and that I had several times read it wrong;
but it didn't strike any deep blow at my identity. But that children
in books called their mothers *Mummy* (or sometimes Mama), not
Mammy or Mam, was something that I never came to terms with
till I was well into adulthood, and that my mother never came to
terms with. As a child, I desperately evolved all kinds of theories
to account for it – I had to, to survive in a book-world. I had some
cousins who lived in London, and when they came to stay with us
I heard them speak. I formed a complicated theory that London
children, for whom mothers must be Mammy or Mam, as they
were for all of us, *spelled* it with a 'u', because they said a 'u' as if
it was 'a'. (How differently we each said 'come'; in Salford we
said it with a deep 'u' sound, but these Londoners said it with an
'a'.) The note of desperation now creeping into my writing is
already reproducing the desperation I felt as a child, going round
in mental circles, trying to account for my exclusion from books,
trying to show I wasn't *really* excluded but that it only seemed so.

I needn't say how wildly involved this theory got, nor how I
evolved a slightly simpler one that turned 'Mama' and 'Papa' into
'Mámma' and 'Páppa' (which was common in my immigrant
street); but I was startled when years later I discovered my seventy
year-old mother (who had been a teacher) had been through the

same desperate attempt to make personal sense out of print by juggling about with sounds, and that she was still doing so! No-one who hasn't experienced this as a child (but surely most of us have experienced it?) realises the sense of your own unreality, your own 'unworthiness' it gives you, and the contortions you must go to, to fit books to your reality, if you are to love them.

It was with this very strong in my mind, that when I started the *Nippers* series I told writers that whatever district they were writing about (and I had already said they must get the shape and tune of sentences right for that district) the word for 'mother' must be the one the children there knew. Early on I got some excellent stories from a teacher, Helen Solomon, about a mining village in Staffordshire. I was surprised to see the children in her stories said 'Mum'. I wrote back, 'I'd have thought they said "Mam".' Surprised at my picking this up, she replied .'As a matter of fact they say "Mom".' 'Then why did you write "Mum"?' 'I thought that's what you're expected to write.'

When five-year-olds come to school without any of the intimate personal building-up-with-words that the book-child has had, they are expected to leap into a language that in sounds, vocabulary, meaning, tune, phrasing, attitude, bears little relationship to their own – *but the pretence is that it is their own.*

The prize for this achievement (beyond keeping their footing in this institution called school) is to be able to read books that bear no relationship to their experience, their longings, joys, fears, and preoccupations – *but the pretence is that they do.* Or rather the pretence is that the children have the same longings, joys, fears and preoccupations as the children in the books, but that their own experience is not 'fit' to be put into books. ('Surely it must be bad enough for them to *have* to drag father out of bed before they go to school, without having to read about it when they get there.') Somehow they are supposed to have the 'right' longings, joys, fears, preoccupations, while having the 'wrong' experience.

It is this *pretence*, that is the most loathsome and demoralising part of our school system, and that stops it being education. For there is something much more important than the fact that spelling and pronunciation don't always match in our language. Book-children, for whom books and words and things-in-print are serious playthings from a very early age, absorb this. No-one is telling them that if they want to read they have to give up all their past experience, and agree that what they have been saying to their Important Adults and their other friends, and what these people have been saying to them, is *wrong*; they simply learn that 'thought' is pronounced 'thawt'. But a child who pronounces 'thought' as 'fawt' – not because he isn't yet old enough to distinguish the sounds, but because this is the language of his community, is in a completely different situation. The whole basis of reading – that print captures what you say – is denied him. 'This is how you write *thought*' we said to the book-child. But to this child we say 'This is how you write *thought* – which you say quite wrongly as *fought*'. He is not learning to read. He is learning a foreign language under the frightening and defeating disability that the teacher pretends it is his own. And he is learning that he, the real person, is not fit to be in books. It is rather like a child in Beryl Gilroy's school who confided, 'There's a telephone in our house, but we're not on it.'

I once, for a short while, helped a man in his thirties to read. He was a market porter, and he had three children (they could read; so could his wife). He had been deaf in one ear since childhood and now he wore a National Health hearing aid – or rather he had been wearing one but it was broken and he was having, of course, to wait months for it to be mended; and the deafness had affected his speech, which apart from this disability was very strong South London cockney. He was an intelligent, very likeable chap, with remarkable patience, responsibility and perseverance. Although he started work at five every morning, he managed on three evenings a week to be down at the library or the baths, learning to read.

He wanted to show me how much he had learned with his previous teacher, and started to read to me, very slowly, from a book designed for teenage remedial groups. It had pictures of cars, and an accident (an old man was knocked down) which had appealed to him as being real experience. I watched his face as he struggled with the word 'yell'. It seemed to me it wasn't just the laborious business of putting three sound symbols together, nor was it the difficulty the double-l presented to a Cockney; rather the word itself was quite meaningless. 'That's *yell*,' I said. 'D'you know what it means?' 'No.'

'Well, what would you call it if I suddenly said very loudly "*Get out of here!*" '

'That's shouting,' he said. I think if this hadn't been our first meeting he'd also have said 'or hollering' (should I write 'ollering'?)

A little while later I was showing him how to pronounce an 'h' by making a bit of paper blow off your hand. (In this first meeting, heaven help me, I got completely bemused at finding myself trying to get John's words to fit the printed page – which meant I had to alter John's words. To alter his words because they had been affected by his deafness was one thing; to alter them because he was Cockney, and his family and his mates were Cockney, seemed quite another. From the very first, I found myself struggling with this problem; how can I help this man to read – which he had *chosen* to do, and which I warmly responded to – without changing his language, which is his identity.) He rather enjoyed this, so I gave him the word 'hug' to practise with. Again, watching his face, it seemed to me it wasn't putting the sounds together, or concentrating on the 'h', that accounted for his expression.

'That's *hug*. Do you know what that means?'

'No.'

'Well what would you call it if I put my arms round you like that, and squeezed you tight?'

'That's a cuddle.'

Now my point is that 'yell' and 'hug' are two very simple words – to a middle-class teacher bending down to a working-class learner. They are short, they are monosyllables, every letter is pronounced, they have distinctive shapes, they relate to gutsy emotional actions; every 'progressive' aspect is covered – except just one: they don't happen to be the reader's language.

This wouldn't so much matter, in fact, if they were intellectual, informative, or clinical words, that could be acquired to cover things that were not one's own direct experience. But hugs and yells do indeed come into John's life, and are indeed important and vibrant to him – only he calls them cuddles, and hollering and shouting (all, incidentally, much more 'difficult' words).

After five minutes of the teenage remedial book, which I'd listened to mainly out of courtesy to John, I'd had enough. I got John to talk about his family, and his work, and his childhood – three things he really enjoyed talking about; and as he talked, I wrote it down – I learned a great deal about the wholesale vegetable market that I knew nothing whatever about, even though it affected my life basically and I depended on it. Schools, if they listened to people like John and his children, would benefit a great deal; for John told me, for instance, that that day he'd seen some people loading into the school-meals van all the rotten stuff that they knew shoppers wouldn't buy – old, sprouting, rubbery potatoes, and such – and he'd had a row with them, because his kids all had school meals, and as it happened that day they'd all come home with upset stomachs, so the content of school meals was much on his mind.

John read what he had said with much more ease and delighted excitement than he had read the printed teenage book. (In his talk, he said 'barrer'. I wrote down for him 'barrow'. He read it out 'barrer' – and he read it in his head 'barrer'. Does this matter? And if it does, *in what way* does it matter?) After a few meetings like this, he began to write his experiences down himself, with me sitting by him spelling words (we wrote them on cards and made a boxful of words he used – 'lettuces', 'porter', 'bloke', 'ticket', 'vegetables' – the second syllable practically disappearing in Cockney pronunciation).

'Greengrocers come down early in the morning to get potatoes, cabbages, sprouts, carrots – all the vegetables. They change all the time; sometimes it's sprouts, or peas, or beans, or cauliflowers. The salesman writes it all down on a ticket, puts the tickets all together on the desk – there might be twenty tickets – and me, my brother, and the other porter load it into the van. I pick one up, I do my barrow-load, my brother does his barrow-load, and the other bloke does his barrow-load. We all work together. We have six barrows – two barrows each.

'I say "Where are you?" He says "Round the Globe" or "Down the Hop". I put the barrow by the van. And sometimes he says "Put them on". So he gives me beer money for that. And if it's enough, I put it on. And if it's not, I say "It's not worth it", and I give it back, and he has to load it himself. . . .'

After three or four instalments written together like this, I suggested he write the next instalment all by himself at home – which he did.

In the course of all this, he brought to one of our meetings his elder daughter's school dictionary which he said he wanted to learn to use. He decided to look up some of the words he'd been saying and writing, that were part of his daily life. He began with 'Brussels'. This wasn't in the dictionary at all. (This was, of course, a small dictionary. If it had been a larger one, it *might* have been in – as a city in Belgium.) I asked John what else his vegetables might have been called, and he suggested 'sprouts'. So we looked up 'sprouts'. (I've rarely experienced before the intense excitement I felt, watching John find his first words in a dictionary ... his finger moving down each column, lingering sometimes, then moving on, passing the word and turning the page, then slowing hesitantly down and turning back ... Over and over again I had to sit on my hands, so that I would not find it for him.) Three consonants at the beginning of a word was very difficult. The first word he turned up was 'spout'. Slowly and laboriously he read out the definition. That was two achievements – to have found a word so much like the one he wanted, and to have read out the definition. But the definition was utterly incomprehensible – even in a dictionary designed for children. So much effort, excitement and eagerness, to be treated so indifferently by educated experts. So I said 'Well, what d'you call that part of a teapot that the tea comes out of?' He was puzzled. 'It's the *teapot*,' he said.

'Yes, but that particular bit. The bit the tea comes out of – what do you call that?'

'It's the teapot.'

'Haven't you got any special name for it?'

'No.'

'Well, that bit's the *spout*.'

He was very interested. 'D'you mean it's the same with a kettle? The bit the water comes out of, that's a spout?'

'Yes.'

What had it done to John, this lack of particularisation in his vocabulary, if it is true that we think with words? (I had always assumed it was true. The note of query slipping in, is due to watching Kit, a baby, without words, who most certainly seems to think, though perhaps he only remembers, and associates.) Had it, just as an example, stopped a mental discussion about teapots developing in him? Could he really think about teapot shape, design, function, performance, if he didn't know that the bit that the tea came out of had its own particular name, and was called a spout? Could he have any strong interest in it, if he didn't know it had a separate name? Yet a baby is interested in every part of his body, and later, moving outwards, in many other things beside, without ever having a name for anything.

Does having names for things mean we can explore and manipulate that thing *in its absence*, doing things with it that even in its presence we can never do to the real thing? Emily was not given her name till she was a few months old; and I remember how frustrated this made me feel, for she lived at the other end of the country and I felt I *needed* a name in order to be able to think about her and hold her in my mind.

But there is much more to this. Some years ago, P. A. Katz, working at Yale University, showed some seven-year-olds and nine-year-olds four similar shapes, then dividing the children into three groups, gave one group a separate invented name for each shape, gave another group one name for two of the shapes and one name for the other two, and gave the third group no names at all. He then tested the children for perception and discrimination between the different shapes. It was very clear that the children who had a name for each different shape could discriminate between them far more easily, and do far more with them. Does the lack of names for them keep our power over things specifically to a baby's level (and what is a baby's level?) And if this is so, *doesn't the refusal by teachers to accept the names a child's particular community gives to things, send that child back to that same level of powerlessness (but with a new anger added, for the personally-acquired power has been taken away by 'educators')?*

We talked about 'spouts' for a while; and we talked about the strangeness of the dictionary definition. And then John in his engrossed way went back to finding 'sprout'. He did find it. After several false trails on his side, and much sitting-on-hands on mine, he found it, and slowly read out the definition. It was something near-botanical. It had never occurred to the compiler that to *every* child who used that dictionary, even including the children of book-families, a sprout was a green vegetable that you ate, or refused to eat, with your dinner. How many educational books *prevent, kill,* education!

As I said earlier, John would talk about his own childhood, write it down, and read it back. His writing and reading were laborious and slow, but at the same time they were very eager and excited. (When he read a 'remedial' reading book, he read far more slowly, and without any excitement at all – only conscientious application.) Because of this, on the third meeting I brought this man whom schoolteachers would say couldn't read or write a copy of Barry Hines' novel *Kestrel for a Knave* (from which the film *Kes* was made – though John had never seen it), and turned to the chapter where a boy describes how he and his friend fill their wellies with tadpoles and he squashes his feet into them. (John's reminiscences of childhood had centred a great deal on days he went camping on a school trip, particularly an exploit when he had discovered frogs.) He read this narrative, which even an educated and literate adult might have had slight difficulty in reading because of the dialect, *quicker* than he had read anything else – in fact, he read it *fast*, making rapid guesses at strange words – and he read it with pleasure, delight and excitement, even though the word 'tadpoles' and its meaning (he didn't *know* about tadpoles; he only knew frogs; I had to explain tadpoles) were completely strange, and on top of everything the idiom (including 'thi' and 'tha' and 't') was broad Yorkshire. Above all, he read it with the completely new discovery that he, John Macadam, South London Cockney, was in a book, this Yorkshire book. We were both tremendously excited.

Some years before I had spoken at a conference in Scotland. A teacher from Glasgow had told me how much the children in her remedial class had enjoyed the *Nippers* stories about the Carter family. 'But aren't they thrown by their London-ness?' I said, for this problem had been very much on my mind, and I felt guilty we had as yet no Scottish stories. 'The places and situations in those particular stories are London, the talk is London . . . Doesn't this bother them?'

'Oh no,' she said. 'The characters, and the experiences, are so real to them – it's the first time they've ever met people they feel they know in books – the first time they've ever read a book right through.'

The dialogue helps, gives extra delighted recognition. But what matters is, you can say 'It's me!'

Going to the right places

One day I went up to the Liverpool Free School. This had been started by John Ord and Bill Murphy in 1971, to provide some educational facilities for the Liverpool kids who were roaming the streets, refusing to attend, or being refused admission to, the state schools; it consisted, at the time I went up, mainly of some adults with teaching experience who liked the kids and had settled in the neighbourhood, some local people who had been rooted there for generations and who offered their various abilities, a large old empty school building given them, after a year of asking, by the local authority, and practically no equipment whatever.

A kid of eleven – a sensitive-looking Irish lad – had just arrived when I got there and said he'd come to learn to read. No-one knew him; no-one knew me, except that the adults knew me by name; we were both newcomers, so we settled down for a little while together. Soon he spoke of a hospital and an ambulance – so many of these kids talk of hospitals and ambulances but they never come into the dyed-in-the-wool infant readers – and I gathered he'd had some sort of an accident, so I suggested he wrote about it. This is that vivid piece, written that first morning spontaneously (though with care and responsibility) for a newly-met stranger who nevertheless was interested in what had happened to him.

> Once wen I nerly got run over and I felt the pain before the
> car hit my head and I could hear the car's brakes skreeching
> and skiding down the road and a man came running into
> the road and stopped the car as much as he could and people

were just staring at me and when the car touched my head
it give me a shiver through my body and my mum batted
me for running into the main road in stead of going to the
zebra crossing.

A little later, two girls came in, also aged about eleven. They'd
been at the Free School a little while, and said they wanted to
practise their reading and writing. Trying to get them to hear in
their heads the conversations in their life and then write them
down, I said to one of them 'Well, what does your mother say when
you come home for tea?' She looked a little blank. 'I don't go home
for tea,' she said. Now I looked a little blank. 'Me mother's at
work,' she said. Then she added, hoping this might help me, 'But
I get her supper when she comes back at night.' What a reversal
of *Janet and John* family roles!
So I asked the two of them if they'd like to write about their
families, and how they spent their day from the moment they got
up. This is what Paula wrote down.

Mary came to wake me up this morning it's better for Mary
to wake Me up Because if I set the alarm clock of it will
wake the Baby up and when she wake up and she wont go
asleep again And when I go over to my Mother I get my
Breakfast then I go up to school I Bring My Dinner Money
with Me – Then Me and come in to the pensioners Room
then we do are English with Marion some-times We do
spellings tests, then when I come we go over to the chipy
and get more dinner then in the afternoon John tacks us to
the picture or the ice ring we were we what to go we can go
and when I come home from school I do the messages then
I have my tea then I mind the Baby if a night while my
sisters works in the pub and why we have to mind the baby
because her mother has to much to do and when I mean she
has to much to do Because when the drain men come my
Brother haves to go down the celer to throw the emty crates
up to the drain Men they threw the full crates down and we
have to check how many crates they have put there is one
man on the lorry one at the top of the celer and one down
the celer then they get a Big long plack down the celer the
man on the lorry through crate the man at the top of the

celer sticked the crate down the plack my Brother stacked all
the crates then locked all the celer up the he give the drain
men a pint of Bitter then when they dranck that they went
Back to the Brewery – so that why I say my sister is to
Bizzy and that's why me and my sisters have turns of each
of mending the Baby and we have to nights each of staying
in then we go out two night and in thown to night I go the
Baths and teach the children to swim a dive and jump in 6 Ft
and she is learning to do the Back div and sometimes I
organise coaches for the kids and we organise one last
Sunday and we went to new feary Baths.

(You may have missed the import of the first sentence. Mary, her
friend, comes *from another house* to wake her up every morning.
Everyone in her own house (she lives in a pub) is already at work.
She can't set an alarm clock for herself because the only other
person in the house is the sleeping baby.)

There is an immense amount here that cries out to be used.
What wonderful satisfying exercises for a class, tossing barrels . . .
and another time miming the movements, the man on the lorry
throwing, the one at the top of the cellar catching and rolling, the
one at the bottom catching, setting upright, and stacking, and all
tipping back a pint at the end, full-stop. . . . The counting and
checking (scope for plenty of games of tricking and catching out
here) . . . the arithmetic of the baby-minding rota . . . the finding
out and co-ordination of the very many different details you need
to organise a coach . . . . There's a wealth of experience here –
unrecognised by most schools. This is what is wrong – most teachers, who are authoritarian, will not recognise the experience of
such a child, will not welcome it and quite informally integrate it
into education. And even the informal friendly ones are stirred by
their own anxieties, and by the honest fact that in some matters
adults are less adequate than children, and in many more matters
teachers are less adequate than working-class children.

When Irma Chilton, a young teacher working in a Welsh
village school, wrote one of the *Nippers* for me – *The Lamb* – she
told me:

Following your suggestion I read the story to a class of
eight- to eleven-year-olds, all, without an exception, farmers'

children. They listened without stirring, which surprised me
as we are always very casual about discipline and have no
formality. I noticed in amazement that a real story should
touch their own experience so closely; the boys especially
following the birth details avidly, hoping, I think, to catch
out the author (who was anonymous); only when the story
was over did the discussion start, because they wanted to
hear the end. The discussion was lively, mainly concerned
with difficult births WE have witnessed and taken part in,
both lambs and calves (some quite horrifying); how WE
make stupid (i.e. stubborn) lambs feed; OUR pet lambs;
lambs I personally have saved. I received a pile of little
drawings done during a wet lunch hour to illustrate the story
– with no prompting at all. My head teacher however,
overhearing part of the reading thought the beginning rather
strong – not beyond the children's experience but he would
have felt embarrassed, he thought, to read it aloud.

As I read her letter, I remembered a conference I had spoken at,
when a Devon teacher told me how he'd moved from a city school
to a village school, and secretly and condescendingly thought
'How dim these children are' – till one day he heard them talking
about what they did *out of school*, and realised that each of them
was responsible for a herd of cows or a flock of sheep, that they
did work he'd never dreamed of, and of which he was utterly in-
capable and ignorant, and on which he and hundreds of other
adults *depended* for life; and he was deeply humble.

Look how Mary, Paula's friend, wrote of her experience:

My mother is small she has BROWN eyes Black Hair. She
Works In a big Factory called the PURAV. She enjoys being
there SHe has many of friends. I have to big brothers WHo
dont work. They try to find Jobs But they can not get one so
we just have to manage with the money we have now. We are
a happy family we have a pet cat called Claw. He is very
playfull. My listtle siter every morning she goes to the baths
she is good a swiming and diving and jumping. Paula my
freand leart her to do these things paula is good at these
things I am not good at these. I am good at writing story's
about adventures. When we go to the beach with the

Chapter 24

> SCHOOL we all LOOK FOR PEBles and PoLiSH they
> come out nice and clean. They look pretty coolours you are
> surpoesed to have a speashel machine to polish the stones
> but I havent got one but the SCHOOL garage has a
> MACHINE wich might do the Job so we will BORROW
> it and poLISH The stones.

Now that *is* education, I found it very moving. 'You are supposed
to have a special machine to polish the stones but I haven't got
one. But the school garage has a machine which might do the job
so we will borrow it.' The school, of course, is the Free School.

Once I went to a local college of education when John Ord was
coming down with some of the kids to explain what the Free
School was trying to do, and to try and raise some money to
continue. The kids often piled into the van with John when he
went off on such trips; it was a great experience for them to travel
from one city to another. John, I noticed, when they arrived and
he gave his talk, was very tired and depressed and evidently
expected nothing. But the children – five or six girls – had discovered the Women Students' Toilet, and behind him, one by
one, with serious and adult faces, they walked off the platform,
on and off and on again, sitting down in between sedately, each
going three or four times during his speech, which had the continued accompaniment of lavatory flushing. When John had
finished, and for the moment all the children were available on
the platform, the Principal, who had invited them, and was
friendly and wanted them to succeed in educational terms, and
had remarked amicably on how John had said they spent time in
many Liverpool buildings other than the school, moved behind
the row of children and asked them in turn, putting his hand on
each head, what sort of places John took them to. 'Bingo', said the
first. 'The skating rink' said the next. 'The chippy', said the third.
'The swimming baths' said the fourth. The Principal was looking
more and more unhappy and nervous. He so wanted them to give
the right answer. 'The library' said the fifth. 'Ah, the library!'
cried the Principal. 'The library!' and he placed his hands warmly
on this child's shoulders and beamed at the audience, begging
them to be kind and tolerant and to like these children who had at
last, as in some television parlour game, given the right answer. (The
audience was mainly bored, disgusted and hostile, and refused.)

Then a woman education lecturer leaned forward from the audience. Speaking with an air of intense capability, helpfulness, and friendliness she addressed one of the children. 'My dear, will you tell us just what you get from your school.' Instead of availing herself of this opportunity to make a pupil's speech on behalf of the Free School, the girl clenched her fists and said 'You leave our John alone!' The lecturer was visibly startled, and so was I. (Hardly anyone else in the hall was listening. They were quite unaware they were witnessing a scene of great educational importance.) 'But all I said, my dear, was – will you tell us what you find in your school?'

'You leave our John alone!' 'My dear, I am not attacking him. I am simply asking you to give us information. . . .' 'You leave our school alone.' 'My dear, I assure you . . . .' This bizarre verbal fight went on for several seconds more. Then the lecturer leaned back with an air of saintly patience, shook her head and said no more.

How was it that this girl knew at once that when those apparently friendly words were spoken she was being *examined and assessed*? And not only she, but her whole team, and primarily her own Important Adult? With great intelligence and spirit – for the contest was utterly unequal, academically speaking – she refused to play. But this wasn't a move that was recognised in the academic game. Within a few minutes, all the students and lecturers, bar a tiny handful, were pushing their way out of the hall.

Of course this girl, who must have been about twelve, had already experienced assessment, and was not fooled by a kind, patient tone; that's why she had truanted, and ended up at the Free School. What filled her with helpless anger now was the feeling that so much – *her life* depended on her finding the right answer (which she knew she couldn't do). It was not surprising these two could not communicate. Where there is assessment there is no communication.

Everyone has *experience* – but teachers *assess* it, say whether it is worthwhile experience (when they agree it happened) or unapproved experience (which is then called no experience, and has not happened). I must repeat this: many teachers in our school system actually *assess children's lives*, and say whether they may have them; they give good or bad marks not for school work but for *lives*.

Chapter 24

Beryl Gilroy, a friend of mine and head of an infant school where she has many nationalities of children, once asked her staff at a staff meeting 'What does culture shock mean to you?' She was given the 'progressive' reply, that it is the shock of the child, etc., etc. And she said 'No. It is the shock of the *teacher*. The teacher who is forced to realise that she must adjust her ideas, and must understand the environment, the culture, the norms of these children. Many teachers cannot stand this.'

She constantly tells her staff to stop 'assessing' the children. At this same staff meeting, which was actually on the subject of 'The "Failure" of children', she suggested that if a teacher had a kid who seems to have a habit of 'failing', the teacher should tell the child 'Whenever you feel you have done something nicely, or learned something new, go and get something you like – perhaps some specially pretty cut-out shape ... whatever you want ... and put it in your own special box.' This was to be the child's own assessment, not the teacher's.

Hers is the only infant school I know where the children appoint the new teachers. Beryl merely chooses the short list. It is also the only infant school I know where a small girl has stood in front of the school at assembly telling a piece of 'news' that so absorbed her that a pool formed on the floor beneath her as she talked and *not one child laughed or pointed or commented in any way*, every child was so hanging on her words. A teacher moved forward and quietly mopped it up, but no child thought it important. What was important was what their school-mate was communicating to them.

In her previous school, where the children first greeted her with remarks like 'Miss, are your knockers black as well?' and 'My Dad says black pussies go the same way as your mouth', the infants, after she had been teaching there a while were doing magnificent writing – thoughts, musing, reminiscences, stories that were perceptive, accurately expressed, full of wonder and curiosity, and founded on a belief that their own identity was matter-of-factly important. She had seven years of this remarkable writing put together, when I first met her; and by a heartbreaking accident someone burned the whole collection – except the pages she happened to have given me to read that weekend. The next chapter consists wholly of this writing that was saved.

Soft nees, hard art

He came at our house – this man wot sed his nam was visitor –
You see he came to have a cup of tea.
You can have tee sed my mum –
Wot wun is it sed the visitor. Tee bags sed my mum.
No fank you sed the man – I never have them tee bags I have
real tee –
wo do you fink you are sed my mum – her voys was all glaree.
Yes who do you fink you are sed me and my brother.
We cudnt make our voys glaree.

Me sister wen on her olidays with her boy friend –
Mum sed Yes let er go – You go slavier isnt all that far –
But one fing Bren, sed me mum – Dont let im jump you – You
are a good class a person.

I went to Hampstead Heath. I sor a man sitting on a seet – He
sed come ere boy – When I wen ner him he had his willie out
– I ran becos me mum sed never stop ner a man with his
willie danglin don.

God is very old. He has been livin in the skies sins the
Dinosars was livin.
His cloes is all torn becos the angels stopt mend in them up.
God has a wife and some kids. The bad one is the devil.

The rag and bone man cam don my road
O clo o o o i he sed
My mum sed that ment have you got fings to frow out
Me dad sed that's a lod of rubysh

Chapter 25

The rang and bone man stopt and me mum gav him sum cloes and he gave us sixpens The rag and bone man had dirty teef and finganils He never cutted them for a fousand years.

Me dad a plice and he ates blk pepul and iris pepul and he tells me mum wot he does to the drunky ones and me mum lafs and so does aunty josey and me gran says Arfur I never knew you was cruel. They are God pepul.

Me mum tryd to give me dad some trip and onyons for his dinner. Me dad sed Yes Rosie we been maryd for 10 years and your dinas is always speshall and hot Me dad kiss her and he had some trip in his mouf.

Me dad buyed a car for 50 punds and it wont go.
Me mum sed you been ad. Me dad sed the man who mad me buy the car will be ad becos me dad was goin round his house to do im.

A leaf is like an oval, a tortoise and an eye could fit into it.
If the leaf could see it wood no wen we was going to pull it off and pick it off. It wood go to sleep and wake up fres and I would lend it me mums eye may cup. A tortoise in a leaf could go to sleep and it would eat the same leaf when it was hungry. When it was all gone it would be back on the grond wher it belongs.

Why cant no one see God God will not show hisself He is old and ugly and his hand and feet walk slow and he is afraid of people and cars and dogs. That why no one can see him. If I see him I will bleeve in him and warsip him. I like some songs what god sed we can sing

I was all alonen in or flat. Then the radiho began to sing – then it talkt, then it sang agen. I was fritened but the radiho person kept quiat for a minit.

The arck was a big boat and Noah and his fings and his famerly went in it.
When they could not get out Naoh said I am fed up. Dove, go and see what is going on. I dont want to sed dove. Then Noah's wif sed You battah go or you won't get no tee. Youre

only a little dove not the cockathewok

My aunty gived me a pund note becos I was good. I wasn't good. Me aunty is soft.

When I wen froo the park, I did a handstand. Can you do that dad I said.
Yes son. Once upon a time I cud.
I stood on my head.
Can you do that dad.
Yes son. Once upon a time I cud.
He always sez once upon a time. Its funny when he does.
When me dad sez once upon a time he begins a story and he keeps it to hisself.

My Auntie Jo got marrid last Saterdy – it was nice My gran starid to cry – me gran-dad sed stop it. You neva crd when you got marrid you was glad to get away from ome. Why dont you think she's the same.

My brother and I have fun. My dad plays with us. We play mothers and fathers. My dad always wants to be the baby. Mu mum is always the little girl and my brother is the mummy and daddy. Its a good game and I like my family.

I dont like it when my mum and dad quarrell. They dont like each other but me my brother like both of them. Me dad cut himself off my mums wedding foto. Me mum sed you black niggah I never should have had you. My dad sleeps with my brother and I go in with mum My dad is kind to us but he tells mum 'Get it yourself' all day long.

Me dad, me mum and me and me brother went to see me grand-dad. It was very nice at grand dads. He is better now. He lives on his owne – my gran dide Me mam huggd him. Come and life wiv me dad she sed All nights I worry about you. Me grand-dad said no. Come and see me wuns a week Rita – that wot I like – you and the kids keep me from deaf and troubl like that God blesh you.

I will never be a teenager when I grow up. I'll just be a man. Teenagers are too bad.

Chapter 25

Me mum was frying a egg for me tea. It dropp on the flour and me mum wen in to get the dus pan to swep it up. When she went the cat ate it off the flour. Me mum said Well I never. She chast the cat out.

I have some fireworks They can be dangerous. We must not tuch them. Sam tells me go and get them but I wont go. I do wot mum says. Me mum does what dad says and so we all do the sam.

A china man came round our house with another man to paint it. They started to paint and the china man fell of the ladder. His friend sed help him. Do somethink. Everyone crowded round. Everyone peeped over. A doctor came and sed go home. The china broke his leg. He was not yellow. Blud cam out of his nose. It was red. It wast even a little bit yellow none of him was. One day I shall see a real yellow one like me dad sed.

Me anty held a egg over the cup and it wen all dribbly just like or dog.

I wunted a tomohak for Xmas. My dad sed that wont do you no good. Why don you have trains and cars. He wunts a tomohak sed my mum. I'll give him tomohak sed me dad Ill give too fick ears. You dont want to think about that me mum told him becaus I'll give you too swlln balls.

My mum was sad becos she betted and er ors didnt win. Your dad will thump me when e niows what I don. Lets go to nans. E cant it me there. When my dad comd there e didnt it er. My mum still cryd. So me dad eld er and sed its don. Lets go ome.

When a teef is in house his art gos hard and his nees go sof and he finks I wl get put in the nick and he has creepy feel and when he comd out his hart gos soft and his nees go hard and he say good I wont get put in the nick.

A buggla cam to Aunty Susy and climd in. Aunty Susy didn't hear the buggla. When she woke up all her things was gone. My mum said its serves you rite becau you keep every thin for your self since mum died. My mum did not send the burgla there but Aunty Susy said she did.

My dad went to a party at his works. He drank vodka and he
was drunk. My mum said servs you right. I hope it makes
you sick. Thats a Rushan drink and you should never drink it
Englis peple should not drink that. Rushan can py sun peple
with there drinks. They are a bad lot always killing and that.
Rushans upset peple and give them bad stummicks when they
dont want to have them.

Some Jews came to live in our flats. I play with ther girl. Her
nam is Rashell. Her mother is always bathin her. My mum said
they are tryin to wash away they sins. God set them wand rin
and they never will stop wandrin.

We ave to eat fish and ships a lot. Dad was sick and mum had
to give back the cookr. We just have to eat fish and ship pie
and fings till later on. My mum will get a job and everything
will be happy. I want to help mum. When I grow up Ill be a
dad and I wont ever be sick and I will have a cookr for my
famly. Las night we was all hungry and then Sally said come
and yous my kitchin.

Wen I went to Jaywic I had a gud time. There was a lot of
water in the sea and lots of sand. We went on it. We left
our cloes. Mums towill got stole and my mum was cross. Her
voyes was cross her face was cross and her hands was cross
becos she dragd us along.

I dont like peple wot alwas go mad – The lady in the grosere
go mad – The school dinnas lady go mad and me sister gos
mad so I dont like peple wot go mad – I feel as if I wan to
be sic when all my frens go mad I feel all untidy and when
they shout ther voys try to tear my cloes rite of.

I ate Dave becs he mite brn down that nic wot my dad is in.
Me dad has a bad foot and he wont be able to run for it.

When Desman comes to slep with my mum I ave to go in the
bath in a bed wot my mum puts there When I fall asleep its
OK but I dont like Desman he comes ever such a lot of nites
to slep and the tap drips.

Ysterday nite I wen to me ante. Me ante laf and laf. Me mum
laf and laf. Me ante sed pic sum flowers I dednot pic any
becoz they was stinking flowers.

Once there was a lady who had flexible arms and legs and
when she sat down her legs would fade away like the ironin
board. One day she went to doctor and said Plis will you
make my legs not flexible or fold away. But the doctor...
(This, sadly, is unfinished ... LB)

There are colours in coal when my mum puts black coal in the
fire – yellow red and dancing flames leap up. I look at the
coal but I do not see the colours. No one can – not even the
queen but they are there all the same. If you wash the coal
you cannot take the colours away. They last for ever after.

My trasure is invisible. I feel it. It is my secret. It comes and
goes at night when I am in bed – just before I go to sleep.
My treasure can be shared with my friends but they don't
know that or they will use it up. I like sharing it with Shirley.
My treasure is a mystery. It lasts just long enough to take me
off to sleep. When I go there I see a Mr Sandman. He pats
his sack and I cuddle my treasure.

Once there was a ghost. It was shut up in a dismal cottage for
every lasting years. One day it said I must have a succulent
lady for my dinner. The ghost waited silently, grinding its
front teeth with hunger. After a while a lady came to the cottage.
This lady is not succulent. She is as thin as a pin but she will
keep me chewing till a juicy morsel comes my way.

We all slept in and my mum didn't give me no porridge this
morning. We went to Eping Forest. It was a long way. My
dads car broke down and we didnt get back till late. We
had a lovely time in the forest and the car went and spoilt
it all. We heard the birds singing and we saw jumping
squirrels rushing through the leaves. We saw a dog who
didnt have an owner. The dog had sad dripping eyes and
its skin was creast over its face. It had long legs and a
stubby tail.

Once there were Ron and Dora and they got married. After
they were married for a little while, Dora got a pain in her
tummy. The ambulance came and she went to the hospital
and had a girl named Carol. After another long wait the pain

came back again the same as before and this time it was Susan
who came. But this was not the end. Dora had pains again.
They were colossal pains and she cried. The ambulance came
speeding and this time Jill was born. After they lived happily
and her pains were gone for ever.

When early man discovered fire he ran to his wife and said
You'll never guess what I ave ere. Its fire and itll burn
you. It's good for cooking, heating and lighting fags. Hold
on to your breath. Dont puff too hard near it. You'll put
it out and then where will we be – shivering and eating
raw meat again. I found this fire and it's going to be mine.
Some one will have to watch it night and day so as to keep
it bright and sparkling.

One day the Inspector came to this school. Two children played
him a record of 'Orpheus'. Then one of them said 'Shall we tell
you a story? . . . Well, the dog bit Orpheus, and chased him into
the overground. And then he had nobody else to bite. So he didn't
know what to do. So he found another dog and they decided to
get married and have lots of babies. And they tried and tried for
a long time but they didn't have any and it was because they were
both boys.' The Inspector went scarlet. Then the other said 'Now
I'll tell you one. Once there was a boy called Prodigal. And when
he came home, Prodigal's father said "Hello, Prodigal". But
Prodigal's brother said "Go away again, you bloody bastard!" '

Unlike many other schools where teachers disapproved of the
experience of such children, *and therefore never discussed it*, in
this school the children's experience was constantly asked for,
and the child helped to put it into accurate words, and it was
sympathetically and respectfully listened to and discussed. Since
language develops with discussions of experience, and since
reading and writing develop naturally in the context of loving and
living, it is noteworthy but not surprising that in the 1969
survey, this school for five- to seven-year-olds, which had a very
large number of non-English children, and which was in a poor
working-class area, beat every other school in the greater London
area, at reading.

Wendy house at the Tate

Meet four people in the world – three children and one adult.

Here is the first child. Age two or three, she came into a railway waiting-room where I sat, with an elderly lady who must have been her grandmother. It was a very large waiting-room with nothing in it but, by some now-empty convention, a very large circular table, and benches all round the walls. Immediately the child invented her first exercise ('game' . . . 'piece of work' . . .). She ran round and round the table four times, then ran to her grandmother and gleefully buried her face in her lap. At this point her grandmother hugged her. Then off ran the child again, stamping her feet as deliberately as a Spanish dancer, experiencing the excitement of shoes, the exhilaration of movement, the satisfaction of the noise one makes oneself, on her next set of four circles. Back to the grandmother again, hug, head down. Then four circles again.

It was just as rhythmic and self-organised as anything an adult might carefully and thoughtfully plot with paper and pencil and numbered diagrams and a background of medical research. Sometimes the granny, when she gave her the hug, would say 'You'll make yourself dizzy and you won't be able to get on the train'; but that was precisely why the child had arranged the hug after every four circlings, her face down in her granny's lap to regain her balance. So she ignored her granny. Her danger point averted by herself, off she ran again.

When she had practised this and perfected this to her own satisfaction she invented a second exercise. This was to run from her grandmother across the room to the bench on the opposite wall, climb it, bounce on it slightly where the slats were evidently loose, crane all her body up so that she could almost, but not quite, kneel on the back of it, look out of the little window that was above the bench, crane even slightly further in order to scrabble with fingertips on the remnants of a coloured sticker on the pane, turn round, jump down (crash!) with both feet carefully placed together, run back to her grandmother. This also she did over and over again, each time exactly repeating the movements and their sequence, and always with tremendous zest. (Many of these movements are in adult-researched books of physical *remedial* exercises for broken-down adults.)

Her grandmother, who was herself very warm, vital, and not at all repressive, evidently began to wonder whether the noise might not bother someone (for by now there were another three or four people in the large waiting room). So the next time the little girl came for the punctuating hug, she suggested she 'played' on tip-toe. This was going to be very difficult. But since the grandmother had throughout affectionately participated, the child was perfectly prepared to co-operate, regarding it as a new exercise. With grave concentrated application, she gathered all her resources for a tiptoe movement, like a tiger gathering itself for a leap. But surprisingly – and *she* was surprised too – she went instead into an up-and-down dipping movement, like a finch in flight. The unexpected non-sequitur puzzled her. She tried it again and again. But the tiptoe movement continued to elude her, and always she went into the up-and-down dip; so she then decided she was not ready for such a development and would try it when she was.

Then she invented her third exercise – to bend low, and walk underneath the table, crouching down with a delighted wonder by the centre leg. She had found her own magic world where adults passed by only from the knee down, non-interfering yet still around her. It was a very sensible place to recuperate, after all the expenditure of physical energy, all the training of muscle and balance and unverbalised counting, and the sincere effort to do what she wasn't quite ready for at another's suggestion. Only she knew when the time to rest had come; only she would know when she could start again.

This was a magnificent playground, yet nothing there had been specially made for a child. It was part of the adult world, available with all its equipment for use, simply because the adult with her was prepared lovingly to integrate with the child, and the community, who were not really bothered, didn't clamp down.

Now here's a twelve-month old. She spent a morning with me. She had picked up a tin that was on a low triangular shelf in the kitchen, having to cradle it in her arms because it was cylindrical and very large for her. She had remembered from a previous visit that there were biscuits in it. I knew she would concentrate enough to get the lid off and that her mother wouldn't be pleased if she ate biscuits, so to distract her I held out a picture of a cat like her own cat, and said 'Look'. Now there were two interesting things pulling her two different ways.

She could have dropped the tin with a crash on the floor, and come at once. But she didn't. She deliberately, without any suggestion from me, went back to the shelf and started to put the tin back on it. This was very difficult for her and took a lot of persistence, not only because the tin was too big for her hands to hold, but also because the shelf was a tiny corner one, with only just enough space for this tin. Finally, after trying many ways to fit it in she managed it by getting the tin on its side. Now it was on its own shelf again. But it immediately started to roll off. Again she could have simply let it crash down, and come running to look at the picture. But she didn't. With great application and effort she managed to turn it on to its base. Then she fitted it in. Only then did this baby come over to me to look at the picture.

During all this it would have been easy, several times, for the baby to have dropped the tin on the floor. It would also have been easy for me to yank her away from the tin in anger and impatience, even to smack her. But I didn't, because, though apprehensive, I was genuinely admiring what the baby was doing, and learning about a baby's skills. And she didn't, because she had parents who respected her and had allowed her the time she needed to explore and finish things, which had enabled her to become responsible and skilful. (An editor, for whose magazine I wrote about this, said 'Responsible At twelve months?' I said 'Yes. Responsible *to herself.*')

The third child I saw in the Tate Gallery, at a Barbara Hepworth exhibition. In the middle of the hall was a large sculpture structure, with steps leading up to it at either end, a sort of roof over it, and holes in the sides. Adults were tip-toeing respectfully

about, gazing and commenting in the 'correct' strained way, tip-
toeing near it, then tiptoeing away.

Into this nervous room came a child of four with father and
mother. The child saw the structure and immediately rushed to
it. She went up the steps, sat on the top one, went inside, peeped
and waved through the holes – which immediately became
windows. Her parents were horrified, though not repressive.
What would people think? In whispered shouts they demanded
the child come out. But she was at home there. They protested,
pleaded, reasoned. But the child stayed, and demonstrated with
unselfconscious delight and assured familiarity that the feared and
mysterious sculpture was – a playhouse. Having played enough,
the child came out and the three moved to another room – the
parents very relieved that the crime was ended. For about two
minutes there was no change in the hall, though you could sense
everyone privately ruminating. Then the first most daring adult
walked, with studied casualness, up to the sculpture, and *went up
the steps*. Someone else followed – still very deliberately casual –
and *sat on the top step*. Someone else went and looked – a little self-
consciously, but trying to pass it off – through a 'window'.

In five minutes, the sculpture was buzzing like a hive. People
were sitting on its steps chatting happily to strangers, leaning out
and talking through the windows, and strolling in and out with an
almost dancing step. All the adults were playing houses – or you
could say they had accepted this sculpture into their world. The
child – unrepressed – had shown them what it was about.

I don't want to labour the point, but you will notice that none
of these children was in a building called School, with an adult
called Teacher, and with equipment specially designed as
Scholastic. They were in the world, with their own drive to become competent in it, and to welcome whatever they met.

As for the adult I said I would speak of, she was a young staff
nurse in a hospital ward where I was a patient. It was visiting-
time, but I had no visitors, so the nurse wandered disconsolately
up to my bed to talk. Sweetly and reproachfully she told me, 'All
they want to do is to go home. As soon as it's visiting time they
ask me, "When can I go home?" ' Sympathising with her hurt, I
said 'But you mustn't think they're ungrateful. Of course they
appreciate all that you've done for them. But – ' and I laughed –
'you know, the real world is outside.' She looked at me, her eyes

glistening with the beginning of tears, and her voice so sweetly plaintive – 'But for us, the real world is *here*!'

I went cold. I wanted to cup my hands and shout down the ward 'Get out all of you! Grab your clothes and get out while you can!'

I sometimes feel like that in a school.

Appendix

I would like more people to know about:

1 The work of Janet Hill, till recently Lambeth's children's librarian, who, among many other lively innovations, in 1973, with her assistant Jenny Evans, advertised for eight people who would be paid £20 a week to read to five Brixton children every day of the summer holidays in each of the children's own homes. It is impossible to write a brief description of this small pilot project that does it justice. I will not even try. But it demonstrated how any person who understands that reading is a warm companionable activity that can only be voluntary, and who enjoys children and adults without any urge to manipulate them, will draw not only the original child but whole families and communities into the delight of books. At least one of these diaries – by Lynne Jones, an office-worker, who was able more than any of the others to carry out Janet's ideas – should be published and widely distributed.

2 The work of Ken Worpole and others at Centerprise, a community centre in Hackney, which to its coffee-bar, bookshop, craft workshop, and play-group, has recently added a publishing-house that publishes books written by local working-class people and sells them in the bookshop where other local people buy and read them. Anyone else can get hold of them too.

3 The work of Jenny Mills and Jean Cox with the Inner Area School Project in Stockwell (the Inner Area Study was a project initiated by the Department of Environment, in which six areas of

Britain were chosen for the study of 'problems'). They encouraged the local school children – infant, primary, and secondary – to believe that by writing about their own district they could put their own stamp on it, even change those parts that were hostile to children. I hope they won't be let down. If they are, I can understand that they won't want to read and write any more. I copied out a great deal of what they wrote because of its perspicacity. This too merits publication.

These are only three activities, that I happen to know about. They all took place in poor working-class districts of London. I would like to write much more about them, particularly the first and third since they have no record, for I found them important and stirring; and perhaps one day, if they are still unrecorded, I will.

There must be many more such happenings all over the country. They have very little to do with reading schemes, or even with school. But they put reading and writing back on its own springboard, and it is vitalised quite simply because it is rooted in life.